THE PAIN AND THE GREAT ONE

GO PLACES!

Judy Blume spent her childhood in Elizabeth, New Jersey, making up stories inside her head. She has spent her adult years in many places, doing the same thing, only now she writes her stories down on paper. More than 82 million copies of her books have been sold, in thirty-two languages. Her twenty-eight books have won many awards, including the National Book Foundation's Medal for Distinguished Contribution to American Literature.

Judy lives in Key West, Florida, and New York City with her husband. She loves her readers and is happy to hear from them. You can visit her at JudyBlume.com, follow @JudyBlume on Twitter or join her at Judy Blume on Facebook.

Books by Judy Blume

The Pain and the Great One: On Wheels!
The Pain and the Great One: Go Places!

The One in the Middle is the Green Kangaroo
Freckle Juice

The Fudge Books

Tales of a Fourth Grade Nothing
Otherwise Known as Sheila the Great
Superfudge
Fudge-a-Mania
Double Fudge

Blubber
Iggie's House
Starring Sally J. Freedman as Herself
Are You There God? It's Me, Margaret
It's Not the End of the World
Then Again, Maybe I Won't
Deenie
Just as Long as We're Together
Here's to You, Rachel Robinson

For older readers

Tiger Eyes
Forever
Letters to Judy: What Kids Wish They Could Tell You

Judy Blume

THE PAIN AND THE GREAT ONE GO PLACES!

Illustrated by
Kate Pankhurst

MACMILLAN CHILDREN'S BOOKS

The Pain and the Great One: Go Places! first published in two separate volumes as
The Pain and the Great One: Going, Going, Gone! 2008 and
The Pain and the Great One: Friend or Fiend? 2008 by Delacorte Press,
an imprint of Random House Children's Books, New York
First published in the UK 2008 by Macmillan Children's Books

This edition published 2015 by Macmillan Children's Books
an imprint of Pan Macmillan
20 New Wharf Road, London N1 9RR
www.panmacmillan.com
Associated companies throughout the world

ISBN: 978-1-4472-3927-7

3 5 7 9 8 6 4 2

A CIP catalogue record for this book is available from the British Library.

Printed and bound by CPI Group (UK) Ltd, Croydon CR0 4YY

To Kamu and Miranda
Who Go, Go, Go!

and

To Emma and Ben Valentine,
my Tashmoo Friends

Contents

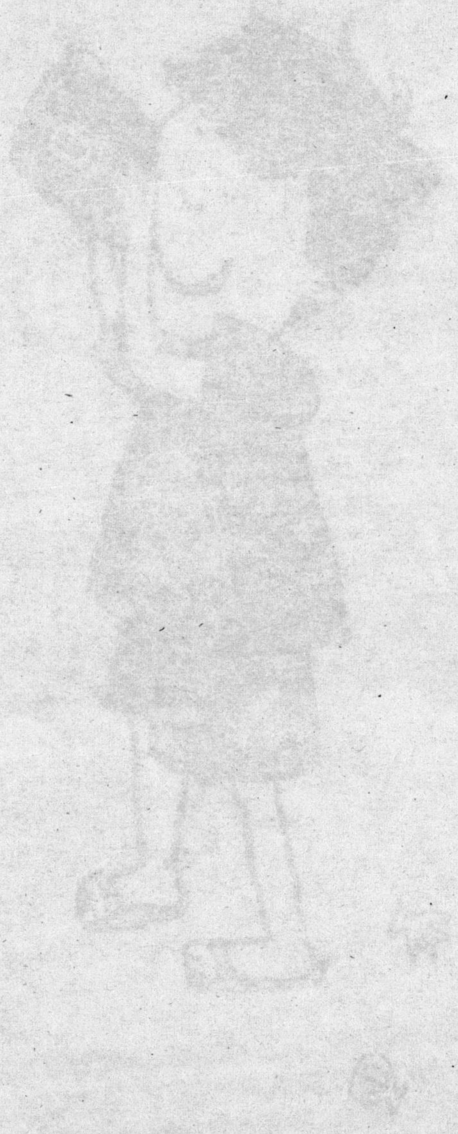

Meet the Pain

My sister's name is Abigail. I call her *The Great One* because she thinks she's so great. She says, "I don't think it, I know it!" When she says that I laugh like crazy. Then she gets mad. It's fun to make her mad. Who cares if she's in third grade and I'm just in first? That doesn't make her faster. Or stronger. Or even smarter. I don't get why Mom and Dad act like she's so special. Sometimes I think they love her more than me.

Meet the Great One

My brother's name is Jacob but everyone calls him Jake. Everyone but me. I call him *The Pain* because that's what he is. He's a first-grade pain. And he will always be a pain – even if he lives to be a hundred. Even then, I'll be two years older than him. I'll still know more about everything. And I'll always know exactly what he's thinking. That's just the way it is. I don't get why Mom and Dad act like he's so special. Sometimes I think they love him more than me.

The Lizard and the Wolf

The Pain

Grandma rented a house at the beach. Yesterday we drove there. I got carsick. I almost always get carsick if the ride takes more than an hour. Under an hour, I'm OK. The Great One doesn't get it. She says, "That doesn't make any sense."

"It makes sense to me," I told her.

"A person either gets carsick or he doesn't," she said. "Look at me – I don't get carsick, which makes me a good traveller."

"Does not!" I shouted.

"Does too!" she shouted back. "Mom, aren't I a good traveller?" Mom was driving. Dad was snoozing in the seat next to her.

"You're both good travellers," Mom said.

"But if you had to choose one of us to take on a trip, wouldn't you rather take the one who doesn't puke every time he gets in the car?" the Great One asked.

"No fair!" I called. "I don't puke *every* time."

"Children," Mom said, "I'm trying to concentrate on the road."

When we got to the beach Grandma took us shopping while Mom and Dad unpacked. We're staying for a week. A week is a long time. Long enough to choose your favourite breakfast cereal. Mine is Cream of Wheat because it's white. I only like white foods. The Great One doesn't care

what colour her food is. She chose Cheerios.

At the supermarket we followed Grandma down the Fun-in-the-Sun aisle. She tossed a tube of sunscreen into our cart. The Great One ran ahead to a display of boogie boards. "I've always wanted a boogie board," she told Grandma. "I could have so much fun in the ocean if only I had one." She looked through the stack of boards. "Oh, this one is so cool!" She held up a purple board. "Isn't this one cool, Grandma?" It had a picture of a lizard on it.

"You think it will be OK with your mom and dad?" Grandma asked.

"Oh yes!" the Great One said. "I'm a good swimmer. You know what a good swimmer I am."

"Well, then – let's get it," Grandma said.

The Great One threw her arms around Grandma. "You're the best grandma in the history of the world!"

Grandma laughed. "Let's hope you think so the next time I say *no*." Then she looked at me. "Would you like a boogie board, Jake?"

"Don't waste your money," the Great One said. "He won't use it."

"Yes, I will!" I said. I chose a yellow board with a wolf's face on it.

The next day, before we headed for the beach, the Great One said, "I hope the waves are big today." Then she looked right at me and said, "I take that back. I hope they're huge!"

At the beach Dad set up the umbrella and opened the chairs. Grandma spread out the blanket while Mom reached into her bag for the new sunscreen. "You first, Abigail," she said to the Great One.

"Why do I have to get sunscreened first?" the Great One asked.

"I thought you *like* to go first," I said.

The Great One gave me one of her *looks*.

When Mom was done with us, the Great One grabbed her boogie board and raced down to the ocean. Dad followed her. I followed Dad.

When I reached wet sand, I stopped. The waves weren't huge. But they weren't small either. I watched as the Great One paddled out on her boogie board. When she got far enough, she turned back and waved to Dad. Then she watched over her shoulder until just before the next wave started. When it did, she was on her board riding in to shore. Then she did it again. And again.

She didn't care if her face got wet or if she fell off her board, or even if she went under a wave. Nothing stopped her.

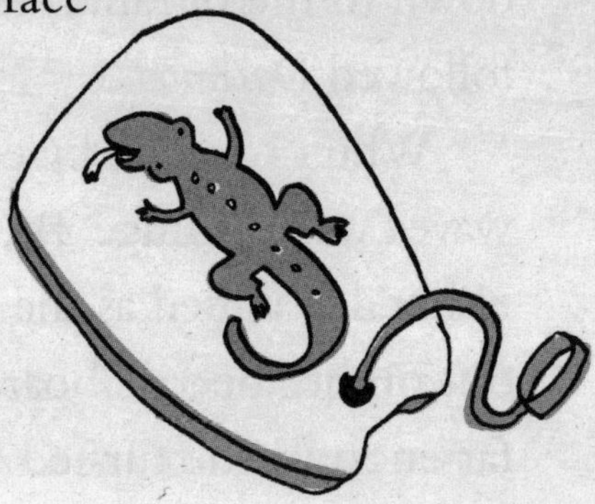

When I got tired of watching, I started digging a hole. I dug deeper and deeper until the ocean came up inside it. Then I sat in the hole. The water was warm. Warmer than in the ocean.

The next day the Great One was at it again. She spent all afternoon in the ocean on her boogie board, riding the waves to shore. She says it's the best fun she's ever had. She says I don't know what I'm missing.

"You *have* to try it, Jake!" she said the next morning while I was eating my Cream of Wheat.

"Try what?" I asked, like I didn't know.

"Your boogie board!"

"I'm waiting," I told her.

"Waiting for what?" she asked.

"The perfect wave."

"Ha!" she said, laughing.

That afternoon I decided to build a sand fort. Grandma helped me. "I have a lot of experience," she said. "I used to help your mom build sandcastles when she was your age."

"With moats around them?" I asked.

"Oh, sure," Grandma said. "They all had moats."

Grandma was good at making turrets and drizzling wet sand on top of them. But after a while she fanned her face with her hat and said, "Whew – it's hot out today. Time for a swim. Want to come in with me, Jake?"

"Not now," I told her. "I have to stay here and guard my fort." I watched as Grandma dived under a wave.

Sometimes I go into the ocean up to my knees. But no higher – not even when I'm with Dad. Because higher means the waves could crash over your head. No way will I ever dive under a wave. Not if I live to be a hundred million years old!

When Mom called us for snacks the Great One said, "You're the only kid on the beach who won't go into the ocean."

"Am not!" I told her.

"Are too!" the Great One said. She was peeling a tangerine. "Do you want everyone to think you're afraid? Do you want everyone to think you're a baby?" She shoved a piece of tangerine into her mouth.

"I'm not a baby!" I shouted, grabbing a juice carton. "I know how to swim in a pool."

"You call doggy-paddle swimming?"

"Yes!"

"Then why don't you pretend the ocean is a big pool?"

"I don't like salt water in my eyes," I told her. "And I don't want it up my nose either!"

"Wear a mask," the Great One called as she ran back toward the ocean with her lizard boogie board.

That night on the boardwalk I saw a store window filled with masks. I asked Grandma if we could go inside. She took my hand and we went into the store together.

I checked out all the masks. I tried on Spider-Man first. Next I tried on Batman. Then I tried on a mask that looked like the president. After that, one that looked like a gorilla.

When Grandma walked away to look at something else, I saw it. The perfect mask – the *Wolfman*! I pulled it on and crept up behind Grandma. Then I poked her in the ribs and growled. Grandma jumped a foot off the floor and shrieked so loud she scared me. Everyone in the store turned to look at us. At least, I think they did. It wasn't that easy to see what was going on from inside the Wolfman mask.

When Grandma calmed down she laughed. "You surprised me, Jake!"

"I could tell," I said.

"Would you like that mask?"

I wasn't going to ask for it, but if Grandma wanted to buy it for me, it wouldn't be nice to say no. So I said, "Sure. Thanks a lot, Grandma!"

"You're welcome, *precious*."

Precious is what Grandma calls me when no one else is around. It's our secret word.

I pulled off the Wolfman mask and plunked it on the counter.

"Getting an early start on Halloween?" the cashier said.

"No," I told him. But I don't think he believed me.

The next day at the beach, after the Great One raced into the ocean, I pulled on my Wolfman mask. Dad said, "That's a scary mask, Jake. I hope you don't scare your sister."

I was hoping I would.

I grabbed my yellow boogie board with the wolf face on it and carried it down to

the ocean's edge. Then I stood on the board, like I was a surfer.

"Look, Mommy," I heard a little kid say. "That boy thinks it's Halloween."

Was he talking about me?

It was hot inside my Wolfman mask. Hot and sweaty. Soon I felt like pulling it off and dumping a bucket of water over my head. Water from the sink, not ocean water.

When the Great One came out of the ocean she said, "Why are you wearing that thing? You look like a dork!"

"I look like the Wolfman," I told her.

"You think the Wolfman wears a bathing suit?"

"He does when he goes to the beach," I said.

"The Wolfman is covered with hair," she said, "in case you didn't know."

"He shaves it off in summer."

She laughed.

So I shouted, "You *said* to wear a mask, remember?"

"I meant a *dive* mask," she said, "not a Halloween mask!"

"That's how much you know!" I told her. "Because this is a . . ." I had to think fast. "This is a *surfer* mask."

"A *surfer* mask?" The Great One laughed again.

"If you don't believe me, just ask the man at the store!"

She was quiet for a minute. "He really told you it was a *surfer* mask?" she said. I knew she was looking at me. I could see her legs but not her face.

"Yes, all the real surfers have them." I was so hot I didn't think I could last another minute inside my Wolfman mask.

"Let me try it," the Great One said.

I pulled off my mask and handed it to

her. It felt so good to be out of it I dumped a bucket of *ocean* water over my head. I was careful to keep my eyes shut.

"How do I look?" the Great One asked. She was posing like a surfer in my Wolfman mask. She looked totally stupid. But I said, "You look cool."

Then she was off, racing out to catch the next wave. But she missed and fell off her board. She fell off on her next try too. And the one after that.

She whipped off the Wolfman mask and came tearing out of the ocean. "This mask doesn't work!" she shouted, waving it in the air. "You tricked me, you little pain! You won't get away with this!"

But I was already racing down the beach, hoping she would never catch me.

Extravaganza

The Great One
Part One

Aunt Diana took us to the county fair. She bought each of us twenty tickets. "I can't believe how much these tickets cost," she said. "Use them carefully."

"We will," I told her.

"I'm going on the Gravitron," the Pain told me as Aunt Diana walked ahead of us, pushing the baby in his stroller.

"No, you're not," I said. "You have to be

at least twelve to go on the Gravitron."

"Ha ha," he sang. "That's how much you know!"

I know plenty about the Gravitron. I know I'm never going on it. It spins around so fast it pins you against the wall while the floor disappears from under you. I learned about it from a TV show called *Amusement Ride Extravaganzas*.

Aunt Diana turned to us and said, "Let's see the farm animals first. Before the baby falls asleep."

The Pain leaned over and whispered to me, "Then the Gravitron!"

The farm animals were in a big barn. First came the pigs. The baby clapped his hands and said, "Uh-oh!" Then came the goats and fancy chickens and rabbits. The baby said, "Uh-oh!" to everything.

When we came out of the barn the Pain poked me. "Time for the Gravitron!"

But Aunt Diana had other ideas. "Let's do the food hall next."

"Is the food hall like the food court at the mall?" the Pain asked.

Aunt Diana laughed. "Not exactly," she said.

The food hall was filled with

homegrown vegetables. The Pain kept running ahead, announcing what was coming next.

"An eggplant that's bigger than the baby!"

"A tomato so huge it could be somebody's head!"

The baby clapped his hands and said, "Uh-oh!"

When we came out of the food hall Aunt Diana sat on a bench under a tree and gave the baby a bottle. The way things were going, I thought we'd never get to the rides. So

I said, "Oh, look, Aunt Diana, there's the Super Slide! The Super Slide is my favourite."

"Mine is the Gravitron," the Pain said, jumping up and down.

"Gravitron?" Aunt Diana said. "What's that?"

"It's where you spin around so fast you're mashed against the wall," the

Pain said. "It's an *extravaganza*!"

"Whoa . . . that's a big word," Aunt Diana said.

"He learned it from a TV show called *Amusement Ride Extravaganzas,*" I explained. "You have to be at least twelve to go on it."

"Unless you're with a grown-up," the Pain told Aunt Diana. "And you'll take me, won't you?"

"I'm sorry, Jake," Aunt Diana said, "but rides give me vertigo."

"Is that like vomit?" the Pain asked.

"Vertigo is dizziness," Aunt Diana said. "Rides make me dizzy, and that doesn't feel good."

"The Gravitron won't make you dizzy," the Pain said. "It only lasts eighty seconds."

"The longer you stand here blabbing, the longer it's going to take on line at the Super Slide," I said, tapping my foot.

"OK," Aunt Diana said, "here's the deal. You two can get on line at the Super Slide. I'll keep an eye on you from here. Then, as soon as I've fed the baby, I'll meet you. OK?"

"OK." I grabbed the Pain's hand and pulled him with me. But on the way to the Super Slide he spotted the cotton candy stand.

"I want blue," he said.

"After the Super Slide," I told him.

"No, now!"

And he used up five of his tickets buying himself a blue cotton candy. I don't like cotton candy. It feels like fuzz in my mouth.

The guy in charge of the Super Slide had a tattoo on his arm. We each handed him four tickets and got on line. I took a swig from my water bottle. It was hot in the sun and the line for the Super Slide wrapped around twice.

"Cotton candy makes me thirsty," the Pain said, watching me drink. "I need water."

"Where's your water bottle?" I asked.

"I left it in the car. Can I share with you?"

"Share my water bottle?" I said. "Ewww, no, thank you."

"But I'm thirsty," the Pain said. "I might die of thirst. Then you'll be sorry."

I didn't answer.

"OK, fine," he said. "I'll go buy a water bottle."

"That's going to cost a lot of tickets," I said. But did he listen? Does he ever listen?

The Pain came back with a water bottle and a toy mouse. "For Fluzzy," he said, walking the mouse up my arm.

"How much did you pay for that?

"Three tickets for the mouse, and five for the water." He chugged down half the water at once. The line for the Super Slide moved so slowly I thought we'd never get to the stairs leading to the top. I checked my watch. Five minutes went by, then ten minutes, then fifteen. The Pain finished his water.

Finally we made it to the stairs. Just as we started to go up, the Pain grabbed my arm. "I have to pee."

"Now?" I asked.

He nodded.

"But it's almost our turn," I told him.

"Can't you wait until we're done?"

He shook his head. "You have to come with me so I don't get lost."

"But we'll lose our place on line." I could see he didn't care. I could see it was getting to be an emergency.

I turned to the girls behind us, who were older than me. "I have to take my brother to the bathroom. Will you hold our place?"

They looked at the Pain. He was shifting his weight from leg to leg. Then they looked at each other. One of them smiled and said, "Sure, we'll hold your place for three tickets."

"Three tickets?"

"That's three tickets *each,*" the other one said. "Because there are two of you."

Then the first one said, "That's six tickets, in case you can't add."

"Hurry!" the Pain said to me.

"Give me three tickets," I told him.

He handed them over. I shoved the six tickets at the girls.

We raced to the Porta-Potties. Another long line. "I can't wait!" the Pain cried.

So I went up to the guy who was next. "We have an emergency situation," I told him.

He looked at the Pain, who was holding the front of his pants. "I've been in a few emergency situations myself," he said. And he let the Pain go next.

When he came out, we ran back to the Super Slide. But when we tried to get through the gate Mr Tattoo said, "Where do you think you're going?"

"Back to our place," I told him.

He shook his head. "Four tickets each, then end of the line, same as everyone else."

"But we already paid! And we stood on

line for twenty minutes!" I told him. "If you don't believe me you can ask those girls at the top of the stairs. We were right in front of them." I called to the girls, "Hey . . ." But they were already sliding down.

"Hey!" I called again when they got to the bottom.

They pretended not to hear me.

"We paid them six tickets to hold our place!" I told Mr Tattoo.

He laughed. "You expect me to believe that?" he said. "Don't you know what happens to children who lie?"

"I'm not lying! And if you don't let us back in, I'm telling my aunt." I grabbed the Pain's hand. "Come on," I said. "We're going to get Aunt Diana."

As soon as we turned away Mr Tattoo called, "OK . . . OK . . ." Then he opened the gate and let us cut the line. "But no more funny business!"

I didn't answer because we were already climbing the stairs as fast as we could. When we got to the top, I looked down. We were so high! I was afraid I'd get *vomitigo* like Aunt Diana. We spread out our rugs, sat on them and, on the count of three, we let go. Whoosh! We slid faster and faster, until it felt like we were flying! Flying over the bumps with the wind blowing our hair and the speed taking our breath away. I heard myself scream. I heard the Pain laugh. And then, just like that, it was over. We were at the bottom.

"Want to go again?" I asked the Pain.

But the Pain had other ideas. And I couldn't get him to change his mind.

Part Two

The Gravitron was off by itself. It looked like a spaceship with flashing lights. The Pain ran ahead of me. When I caught up to him, he was in front of the sign that read 6 TICKETS PER RIDE. NO ONE UNDER 12 ALLOWED UNLESS ACCOMPANIED BY AN ADULT.

The Pain searched for his tickets. He turned his pockets inside out. Finally he cried, "I have no more tickets!"

I could have told him that. If he hadn't wasted his tickets on blue cotton candy, a water bottle and that mouse, he'd still have thirteen tickets left, like me. "Here," I said, handing him six tickets. "Have a good time. I'll wait for you."

He couldn't believe I forked over six tickets just like that. But I knew my tickets were safe. I knew they weren't going to let him go by himself.

The Pain took the six tickets up to the woman in charge. She had spiky purple hair. "What's this?" she asked.

"It's six tickets to ride the Gravitron," he said.

She tapped the sign. "No one under twelve without an adult."

"I'm not under twelve," the Pain told her. "I'm just small for my age."

Purple Hair laughed. "Come back in ten years," she said.

"Everyone in my family is small," the Pain argued. He pointed at me. "Look at my aunt Abigail . . ."

Oh, great! I thought. Now I'm supposed to be his aunt.

Purple Hair looked over at me. "I'm supposed to believe *she's* your aunt?"

The Pain stood behind her making signs at me. So I stood as straight and tall as I could and gave her the *evil eye*. I don't

know what the *evil eye* is exactly, but I once read about it in a scary book.

"I told you we were all small," the Pain

said. "And it's not nice of you to make fun of small people."

While the Pain and Purple Hair were arguing, a long line of teenagers were handing her tickets and piling into the Gravitron.

Then I heard Aunt Diana calling, "Abigail, Jake! What are you doing here? You were supposed to wait for me."

"We are waiting. We're waiting here at the Gravitron!" the Pain told her.

Purple Hair checked out Aunt Diana. "Are you the mother?"

"I'm his aunt," Aunt Diana said.

"My *other* aunt," the Pain said.

Aunt Diana looked confused. But before the Pain could explain, a big guy came by with a couple of teenage boys. "Diana!" he called.

Aunt Diana looked up. "Rick!" she

sounded surprised. She whispered to us, "It's my boss!"

"What are you doing here?" Rick asked.

"I'm with my niece and nephew," Aunt Diana told him. "What about you?"

"I'm with my son and his friend."

In less than two seconds the Pain made his move. He tugged on Rick's arm. "Will you take me on the Gravitron? It only takes eighty seconds. I'll give you all my tickets if you do."

I didn't remind him that he had no more tickets. Or that he owed me six.

"Jake," Aunt Diana said, "it's not polite to ask—"

But Rick stopped her before she finished. "No, it's OK. Maybe this will prove to my son I've still got what it takes." He handed Purple Hair the tickets. Then he took the Pain's hand and they disappeared into the Gravitron.

"Uh-oh!" the baby said.

I was thinking the same thing.

The Gravitron started turning, slowly at first, then faster and faster, until it was whirling. The flashing lights blurred into a hundred colours. The music played louder and louder.

I wondered what it was like inside. I wondered why I was scared to try it but the Pain wasn't. He's afraid of the ocean and I'm not. He still sleeps with his stuffed elephant. He gets carsick! He's probably going to get sick from the Gravitron too. They'll probably have to carry him out.

Eighty seconds later the Gravitron slowed down. Then it came to a stop. The teenagers piled out. Some of them were laughing like crazy. Some of them lined up to go again. One girl was crying. The last ones to come out were Rick and the Pain. The Pain was smiling. But not Rick. Rick's face was pale. He was holding his chest.

"Rick!" Aunt Diana cried. "Are you all right?"

Rick sat down on a bench. "Just give me a minute." He took some deep breaths. Aunt Diana handed him her water bottle.

He took a long drink. "Do you know what it's like in there?"

"I've no idea," Aunt Diana said.

"Believe me," Rick said, "you don't want to know."

I pulled the Pain aside. "What was it like?"

"It was an *extravaganza*!" He jumped up and down.

"And you didn't get sick?" I asked.

"Why would I get sick?"

Then Aunt Diana called, "Jake, come over here."

I followed him over to Aunt Diana. The baby clapped when he saw us.

Aunt Diana said, "Jake . . . don't you have something to say to Rick?"

At first the Pain didn't know what he was supposed to say. I could tell by the look on his face. Then he started smiling and dancing all around. "Hey, Rick . . ." he called, "want to go again?"

The Furry Booger

The Pain

We have a pussy-willow tree behind our house. Justin and Dylan came over after school today and the three of us picked pussy willows. We took off our shoes and socks and stuck pussy willows between our toes. They felt soft and tickly. We tried walking around without losing them. Then Dylan picked another pussy willow. "Watch this!" he said, and this time he stuck it up his nose.

Justin said, "Don't do that!"

"Why not?" Dylan asked. "I can blow it out any time I want." He held his other nostril shut and blew until the pussy willow came flying out.

That made us laugh.

"See? I told you," he said. He picked another pussy willow and stuck it up his other nostril.

So I picked a pussy willow and stuck it up my nose.

"Come on, Justin . . ." Dylan said.

"Oh . . . OK," Justin said. And he did it too.

We decided to have a contest to see who could blow their pussy willow the furthest. We made a line with a couple of sticks and stood behind it. Then all three of us blew at once. Dylan's pussy willow flew out and landed on the other side of our line. Justin's came out, but it just dropped to the ground and lay there next to his foot. I blew and blew but nothing happened.

"Try again," Dylan said.

So I did. Still nothing.

"Let me look," Justin said. He looked up my nose, then shook his head. "I don't see anything. Are you *sure* it didn't come out?"

"I can feel it," I said. "It's like having a big furry booger up my nose."

Dylan and Justin laughed. But I didn't. Justin said, "Get your magnifying glass, Jake."

"Can't," I told him. "I gave it to my sister."

"Go ask your sister if we can borrow it," Justin said.

"You come with me."

So the three of us went inside and up to the Great One's room. Fluzzy was curled

up on her bed. He sat up when he heard us. The Great One was at her desk, cutting pictures out of a magazine.

"We need to borrow the magnifying glass," I told her.

"What for?" she said.

"We have to study something." I looked at Justin and Dylan. They nodded.

"What?" she asked. "What do you have to study?"

"We need to study a pussy willow," I told her.

She slid open her desk drawer and took out the magnifying glass. "Give it to me."

That made Dylan and Justin laugh.

The Great One looked over at them. "What's so funny?"

Dylan covered his mouth and Justin looked up at the ceiling.

"I don't have all day," she said. "I'm a very busy person. So either hand over the pussy willow or go away."

"It's in a . . . in a . . ." I started to say.

"In a *what*?" She looked at me. Now she was really interested.

"It's in a private place," I whispered.

"I'm not letting this magnifying glass out of my sight," the Great One said. "If you want to use it, you have to show me the pussy willow."

Before I could say anything, Dylan blurted it out. "He can't show you. It's up his nose!"

"Your nose?" the Great One said, looking at me. "Ewww . . . that's the most

disgusting thing I ever heard! What's it doing in there?"

"It's stuck!" Justin called.

"You have a pussy willow stuck up your nose?" she asked me.

When I didn't answer she dashed into the hall calling, "Charlie . . . Charlie . . . come quick!"

Charlie is our babysitter. She's on the track team at her college. In two seconds she was up the stairs, sweeping everything out of her way, including Justin and Dylan. "What's the problem?"

"The Pain has a pussy willow stuck up his nose!" the Great One told her.

"What?" Charlie said, like she must have heard wrong.

"A pussy willow . . . stuck up his nose!" the Great One repeated.

"Can you blow it out?" Charlie asked me.

"He tried," Justin and Dylan said together.

"I tried," I told Charlie.

Charlie flew back down the stairs. The rest of us followed. Fluzzy took a flying leap off the bed. Maybe he thought we were playing a game and he didn't want to miss the fun. Only *I* knew it wasn't going to be any fun. Not for me.

In the kitchen Charlie whipped out Mom's emergency book, the one with all the numbers and lists. She called Dr Bender's office and told them I had a pussy willow stuck up my nose. Then she listened. When she hung up, she said, "Dr Bender's not in the office today. His nurse said we should go straight to the ER."

"That means emergency room!" Justin sang. He sounded excited. Like we were going to a magic show.

"I went to the emergency room once,"

Dylan said. "When I broke my foot." He sounded like he was going to the same show.

"And that's where I got my stitches!" The Great One pulled up one leg of her jeans and showed us her scar. "Fourteen of them," she said proudly, like it was the most fun she ever had.

"I don't want to go to the emergency room!" I told them.

"You should have thought of that before you shoved a pussy willow up your nose!" the Great One said.

"I need Mom," I told Charlie.

"I'm calling her cellphone right now," Charlie said.

But Mom didn't pick up, so Charlie left a message.

"I need Bruno," I said, heading upstairs.

At the ER we waited. We waited and waited and waited. Babies cried. People coughed. Somebody moaned. The Great One played Go Fish with Justin and Dylan. I leaned against Charlie and said, "Where's Mom?"

"She's on her way."

"When will she be here?"

"Before it's your turn."

But then it *was* my turn and Mom still wasn't there.

They put me on a table with wheels and pulled white curtains all around. Charlie came inside the curtains. The Great One followed her. Justin and Dylan stood outside, peeking in.

The doctor wore blue scrubs with a white coat over them. She had a stethoscope around her neck. “I’m Dr Itchee,” she said.

"That's a funny name," I said.

She stuck a thermometer in my ear.

"I don't have a fever," I told her.

"It's routine," she said. Next she grabbed one of those doctor sticks. "Open your mouth and say, 'Aaah'."

"I don't have a sore throat," I told her.

"It's routine," she said. Then she put the ends of her stethoscope in her ears. "Now let's have a listen."

I started to say, "And I don't have a . . ." but she said, "Shhh . . ."

After that she wanted to feel my belly. I felt like shouting, "The pussy willow is up my nose!" But I didn't. Instead I told Charlie, "I want my mom."

"I know it, sweetie." Charlie petted my head like I was Fluzzy. She doesn't have permission to call me *sweetie*. Only Mom is allowed to call me that.

But I was glad she was there, so I didn't say anything. I didn't even tell the Great One to take her hand off my arm.

Next Dr Itchee said, "Can you lie back and hold very, very still?"

"Maybe," I said.

Dr Itchee pulled on doctor gloves. I held Bruno against me. I was scared but not *that* scared. First Dr Itchee looked up my nose with a light. "*Aha!*" she said. She sounded like the magician who came to Dylan's birthday party. He was always saying "Aha!"

"It's really up there," Dr Itchee said. She put her light away. "OK, Jake . . . I'm going in now." It sounded like she was going to shrink herself into a teeny, tiny doctor and crawl up my nostril.

But then I saw the long, pointy tweezers heading for my nose and I shoved them out of the way. "No!" I yelled.

Dr Itchee said, "I can't do this unless you keep still."

"He's scared," the Great One said.

"I think this might be easier if you both waited outside," Dr Itchee said to Charlie and the Great One.

"But I *need* them!" I told Dr Itchee. "They have to stay."

"All right," Dr Itchee said. "But your sister has to be quiet. Can you be quiet?" she asked the Great One.

I would have laughed except I was too scared. For once the Great One didn't say anything. She just nodded.

"This won't hurt if you hold still," Dr

Itchee told me. "And it will only take a minute. That's sixty seconds. Can you count to sixty?"

"Of course he can count to sixty!" the Great One said. "He's in first grade."

Dr Itchee shot the Great One a look. The Great One covered her mouth and said, "Oops!"

I held on to Bruno and squeezed my eyes shut.

Then Dr Itchee said, "You can start counting now. Don't forget to say 'one hundred' between each number."

The Great One counted with me. "One – one hundred, two – one hundred, three – one hundred." I felt something cold inside my nose. I held Bruno tighter. "Four – one hundred, five – one hundred, six – one hundred . . ."

Then I felt the cold thing come out of my nose and Dr Itchee said, "Got it!"

That's when Mom came rushing in with Dylan and Justin right behind her. Mom gave me a big hug.

"Sweetie," she said, "you're so brave!"

She kissed me and kept patting my head.

"He's not *that* brave," the Great One said.

Justin and Dylan gave me high fives. Then Dr Itchee sat on the edge of my table.

"OK, boys," she said. "I want you to listen carefully to what I'm going to say." She looked from Dylan to Justin to me. "Are you listening?" she asked.

We all nodded.

"Never, and I mean *never,* put anything

customerservice@waterstones.com
or 0808 118 8787.

Buy online at Waterstones.com or Click & Collect. Reserve online. Collect at your local bookshop.

Did you love the last book you read? Share your thoughts by reviewing on Waterstones.com

Waterstones

Refunds & exchanges

We will happily refund or exchange goods within 30 days or at the manager's discretion. Please bring them back with this receipt and in resalable condition.

Waterstones

19 King Street
Twickenham
London
TW1 3SD
020 8744 2807

* GIFT CARD RECEIPT *

Value Redeemed	£5.99
Card No	*** **** **** **** 7804
New Balance	£9.53

****
PLEASE NOTE - THIS IS NOT A GIFT CARD
Please keep with your gift card
****

STORE	TILL	OP NO	TRANS.	DATE	
0726	2	726001	205231	10/08/2018	15:09

Waterstones

19 King Street

Twickenham

London

TW1 3SD

020 8744 2807

SALE TRANSACTION

PAIN AND THE GREAT	£5.99
9781447239277	
Balance to pay	£5.99
Gift Card Tendered	£5.99

VAT Reg No. GB 108 2770 24

STORE	TILL	OP NO.	TRANS.	DATE	TIME
0726	2	726001	205231	10/08/2018	15:09

9990207260022052316

up your nose that doesn't belong there."

"What belongs there?" Justin asked.

"Maybe nose spray," Dr Itchee said. "But only if the doctor prescribes it. And never put anything in your ears either. Not even a Q-tip."

"How about between your toes?" Dylan said.

"Between your toes is OK," Dr Itchee said. "There's no place for it to get lost. But never put anything in any of your bodily orifices."

"Body *offices*?" I started thinking about having offices inside my body. And every day tiny people would go to work there.

"Orifices," Dr Itchee said.

"They don't know that word," Mom told her.

"Even *I* don't know that word," the Great One said, "and I know a lot of words."

"It means openings," Dr Itchee said. "And in this case it means bodily openings."

"You mean holes?" Justin asked.

"Yes," Dr Itchee said. "Nothing goes in any of your—"

"Holes!" Dylan sang. Then the three of us laughed.

Dr Itchee sighed. "Let's call them bodily openings, OK?"

"What about food?" Justin asked. "Food goes into your mouth and that's a—"

"Hole!" Dylan sang again.

Mom said, "Boys – listen to Dr Itchee. She's trying to tell you something important."

"Thank you," Dr Itchee said to Mom. "Jake was lucky today. But I've seen kids who weren't so lucky. So I want you all to promise you'll never do that."

"I promise," I said.

"Me too," Dylan said, "even though it was a fun game!"

Justin said, "I already knew not to put anything up my nose, because my dad's a doctor."

Dr Itchee looked surprised. "Then why did you do it?"

Justin shrugged. "Because my friends did."

"Just because your friends do something doesn't mean you should."

Justin's face turned red. He looked like he was going to cry. Mom said, "I think Justin knows that now. I think they all understand. Right, boys?"

We nodded. Then I said, "Can we go home now?"

Dr Itchee said we could.

"And can I take that furry booger with me?" I asked.

"Ewww . . ." the Great One said. "That would be *so* disgusting!"

"I like being disgusting," I told her.

"And you're really good at it!" she said.

"Thanks," I answered.

"You're not welcome."

I laughed with my friends. Then we all went out for ice cream.

Kapooie One

The Great One

Yesterday it snowed. The first snow of the season. We built a snowman and put Dad's old rain hat on top of his head. But last night it rained and made a mess of the snow. It's still raining. A rainy December Sunday. Not that Dad's rain hat is helping our snowman.

I watched out the window as he melted away.

When he was just about

gone, Dad called, “Who wants to go to a movie at the mall?”

“I do,” the Pain shouted. “I want to see *Fried*.”

“No fair!” I said. Because who wants to see a stupid movie about a bunch of robots trying to fry each other? “I want to see *Unicorn*.”

"*Unicorn*?" the Pain said. "That's a *girl* movie!"

"Is not!" I told him. "It's about two boys and a girl."

"But it's still a *girl* movie!"

"We'll only go if you can compromise," Dad told us.

"What's compo . . . what's that word?" the Pain asked.

"Compromise," Dad said. "It means decide together. It means if Abigail wants red and Jake wants blue . . ."

Before Dad could finish I called, "We choose purple!"

"Good thinking, Abigail," Dad said.

I smiled. I like being a good thinker.

Then Dad added, "But that's not necessarily the way it works, because maybe there is no purple. Maybe you have to decide on either red or blue because those are the only choices."

"I know," I said to Dad. "You can take the Pain to see *Fried*, and Mom can take me to see *Unicorn*." I knew *that* was good thinking!

But Dad said, "Mom needs the afternoon off to catch up on work."

"OK," the Pain said, just like that. "I'll see the unicorn movie."

"You will?" I asked.

"Yes," he said. "Because I'm a good compo . . ."

"Compromiser," Dad said.

That made me mad. "How come you didn't give me the chance to prove what good compromiser I am?" I asked Dad.

"I'm sure you'll have the chance to prove how well you can compromise very soon." Dad checked his watch. "Go and

get ready. We'll have lunch at the food court."

"Yay, the food court!" the Pain shouted. "I want pizza!"

"I want burritos!" I shouted louder.

"Pizza!"

"Burritos!"

"Children," Dad said, "it's time for another compromise."

"So soon?" I asked.

"I told you you'd get the chance to prove how well you can compromise," Dad said to me.

But before I could say anything, the Pain sang, "OK, I'll have burritos."

"Yay . . . burritos!" I sang.

"Not so fast, Abigail," Dad said. "You got to choose the movie. Jake gets to choose which kind of food to have."

"But, Dad . . . he only eats white food. Doesn't that make it unfair?"

"There's no restaurant in the food court that serves only white food," Dad reminded me. "So I don't think you have to worry about that."

The Pain was smiling that sly smile of his.

"OK," I said. "Pizza."

The Pain shouted, "Yay . . . pizza!"

The mall was crowded. Holiday music was playing and there were decorations everywhere. A big cardboard Santa held a sign pointing to Santa's Workshop. That reminded me of something. So I started telling Dad this story about when I was little and Aunt Diana took me to Macy's to see Santa and I cried because when I sat on Santa's lap he kept *ho-ho-ho*-ing in my face and he had the most disgusting breath ever.

Dad said, "Was Jake there too?"

Shoes
Santa's Workshop

"Jake isn't in this story," I said.

"Who wants to be in your boring old story?" the Pain mumbled.

My story got longer and longer because one thing led to another and Dad finally said, "How does this story end, Abigail?"

And I said, "It ends . . . it ends when . . . um . . ." And then I looked over at the Pain but he wasn't there. I turned and checked behind me. He wasn't there either. I looked all around. But he wasn't anywhere. So I tugged Dad's arm and said, "Where's the Pain?"

"I thought you said Jake isn't in this story."

"Dad – I mean he's gone. One minute he was next to me and then *kapooie* – just like that, he wasn't."

Dad looked in every direction. Then he

ran up and down the mall, calling, "Jake . . . Jake . . . where are you?"

I tried to catch up with him. "Dad . . . wait!"

By then Dad had found a security guard. "My son!" Dad said. He sounded out of breath. "My son is missing!"

The security guard went into action, pressing numbers on his walkie-talkie. "Don't worry, sir," he said to Dad. "We deal with this all the time."

"His name is Jake," Dad told the security guard. "He's six years old."

"He'll be seven in April," I added.

"He's missing his top two front teeth," Dad said. "He has brown hair and brown eyes, and he's wearing a . . . a . . ."

I finished for him. "A grey sweatshirt with a big kangaroo on the front. Aunt Diana brought it back from Australia, and . . ."

Before I could finish telling about the Pain's clothes we were at the security station. Mom's told us a million times, if we ever get separated at the mall, we should tell a security guard. She says he'll take us to the security station and that's where she'll come to find us. Maybe the Pain forgot our plan, because he wasn't there. And no one had heard anything about a boy who was lost.

Suddenly I heard a man's voice over the

loudspeaker. "Attention, shoppers! We have a missing six-year-old boy last seen near Toy City. If you see him, notify security immediately." Then he described the Pain. After that he said, "Stay where you are, Jake. We're going to find you."

"Try to stay calm, sir," another security guard said to Dad.

I wanted to tell him my dad is always calm. I wanted to say there's no one in the whole world who's more calm than my dad! But I didn't. Because I could see in Dad's eyes that he was worried. And seeing Dad that way was scary. If I was the one who was lost, Dad wouldn't be worried. He'd just say, "Abigail, we missed our movie because of you."

Now there were security guards everywhere, and regular police too. I could see them from the window of the security station. Some of them were driving around in carts. And the loudspeakers didn't let up.

"We'll find him," the guard told Dad.

"I know we will," Dad said. "We have to."

And then you can tell him what a pain he is! I thought. And how he made us miss our movie! I didn't actually say any of that out loud. Because I started to think of the Pain being lost and scared. Then I got scared and grabbed Dad.

"It's going to be OK, Abigail," he said.

"Promise?" I asked.

He hugged me. "Promise."

Kapooie Two

The Pain

The Great One's story was so boring I stopped listening. When we passed Toy City I saw a big crowd. I wondered what all those kids were looking at. I wiggled my way up front to see. And there it was – a giant robot made of Lego, walking up and down in the window. I pressed my face against the glass. That robot was way bigger than Dad. That robot was huge! It was incredible. It was the most incredible

Lego toy ever! "Can you believe it?" I said to the Great One. "Don't you wish someone would give you *that* for Christmas or Hanukkah?" We're lucky because we have a Christmas grandpa and a Hanukkah grandma.

The Great One said, "Yes, I would like that Lego set. How about you? What else do you wish you could have?"

I looked up then, because that voice didn't sound anything like the Great One. And when I did I got a big surprise – because it *wasn't* the Great One! It was some other girl. She was maybe in fifth grade. "You're not my sister!" I shouted.

And she answered, "Did I say I was?"

"No, but you're talking to me," I told her.

"You talked to me first," she said.

"I wasn't talking to *you,*" I said. "I was talking to my sister."

BIG
BOT
$

"Fine," she said. And she walked away.

I thought the Great One was right behind me, with Dad. But when I looked around I didn't see them. Probably she and Dad were inside the store. So I went in too. It was crowded. I felt like I was swimming through an ocean of legs. Legs and shopping bags and raincoats and dripping umbrellas. I pushed my way through the store, but I couldn't find Dad or the Great One.

I knew the food court and the movies were upstairs. So I got on the Up escalator. I'm not supposed to go on the escalator without holding hands. But I did it anyway. And when I got off I stood at the top and looked around. No one was watching so I decided to go for it. I decided to do something I've always wanted to try. I walked *down* the Up escalator. And nothing bad happened! Some people looked at me, but nobody said anything.

Then I rode it back upstairs.

When I got off the escalator this time, I saw the bookstore. They must be in there! I thought. We always stop at the bookstore when we're at the mall. So I raced through the store until I came to the children's section. I was sure I'd find the Great One sitting in the red beanbag chair with a pile of books. Instead, who was there? The girl from Toy City. *She* was sitting in the beanbag chair, reading.

"My sister likes that book," I told her.

She looked up. “You again!” she said. “Are you following me?”

“No,” I told her. “Are you following me?”

“How could I be following you when I was here first?”

I didn’t answer.

“Where is your sister anyway? How come she’s not with you?”

“I don’t need her!” I said. “I know where the food court is and I know where the movie is too.”

“You’re going to the movies?” she asked. “So am I. What are you going to see?”

“It’s a compo . . . it’s a compro . . .” I started to say. But I couldn’t remember that word.

“Never heard of it,” she said. And she went back to her book.

I left the bookstore and looked around.

I was angry at Dad for getting lost with the Great One. He should know better. I started to feel funny then. I could feel the *thump*, *thump*, *thump* of my heart. And a big lump in my throat.

Suddenly I heard a voice coming from everywhere. At first I thought I was dreaming, because it sounded like Dad. "Jake . . . don't worry, son. We'll find you. You won't be lost for long." It *was* Dad!

"I'm not lost," I said. "You are!"

Dad kept talking. "Don't go anywhere with anyone."

"OK," I said.

"If you're in a store, tell a salesperson or a cashier who you are. And they'll know what to do." Dad said.

"OK," I answered again, thinking he could hear me the way I could hear him.

I went into the nearest store. It was the skate-and-surf store. The music inside was so loud I had to shout at the guy behind the counter. "Hi, I'm Jake."

"Hey, dude," he said to me.

"You know what to do, right?"

"Sorry, dude, I'm really busy right now."

"Should I wait?"

"Up to you, dude."

I decided to go up to the cashier instead.

"I'm Jake," I told him.

"Cool name."

"My dad's looking for me."

"Don't worry, dude. Your secret's safe with me."

What secret? "Maybe I should go to another store," I said.

He shrugged. "Whatever."

When I came out of the dude store I saw the lights spelling out PIZZA. I ran up to the counter and I said, "I'm Jake."

"What'll you have, Jake?" the server man asked.

"You're supposed to say you found me," I told him.

"OK, sure." He snapped his fingers like he was a magician. "I found you!"

I told him, "No, not like that."

"What is this?" he asked. "Some kind of knock-knock joke?"

I heard Dad's voice again. "Jake . . . Where are you, Jake?"

"At the pizza place," I said. "I'm hungry, so I'm going to eat, OK? You said we could have pizza."

"Yeah, sure, kid," the server man said. He thought I was talking to *him*. "What'll it be?"

"I only eat white food," I told him.

"So you want a white pizza?"

"OK."

"We'll call you when it's ready."

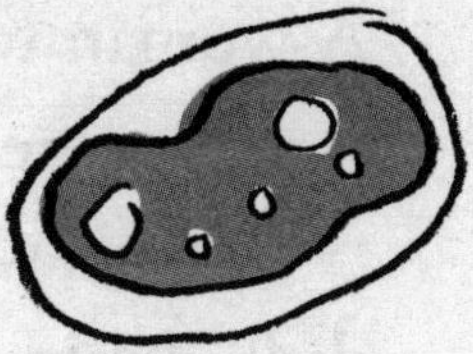

"My name is Jake."

"Yeah, you already said."

Then I heard another voice saying, "Jake is six years old. He's wearing jeans and a grey sweatshirt with a kangaroo on it. He has brown hair and brown eyes. He's missing two front teeth. Please stop a police officer or a security guard if you spot Jake."

I sat down at a table to wait for my food. And suddenly three big girls surrounded me. They started jumping up and down. "It's him! It's him! You're Jake, right?"

"How do you know my name?" I asked.

"They're only blaring it all over the mall," one of them said.

Then another one shouted, "We found him! We found Jake!" And she waved her arms around.

More people made a circle around me.

A woman with curly hair called, "I'll watch him. You get security!"

That's when I got scared. "I want my dad!" I said.

"He wants his dad," they repeated.

"And my sister," I said.

"And his sister," they repeated, like we were doing a play.

"Don't worry, Jake," the woman with the curly hair said. "They'll be here soon."

Then the girl from the bookstore inched in close to the curly-haired woman. She looked at me. "Why didn't you *say* you were lost?"

"I wasn't lost!"

"Do you two know each other?" the curly-haired woman said.

"Not really," the girl said.

"Vera, this is Jake," the curly-haired woman said. "Jake, this is my daughter, Vera."

"I want my dad!" I said again. I thought about crying.

But then Dad was pushing through the crowd. The Great One was right behind him, shoving people out of her way. When Dad spotted me, he called, "Jake!" I jumped up from the table and ran to him. He scooped me up and kissed me a hundred

times. He held me so tight I could hardly breathe. But I didn't care.

When he put me down the Great One said, "Why did you do that?"

"Do what?" I asked.

"Get lost," she said.

"I didn't get lost. You and Dad got lost."

"That's crazy," she argued. "You lost us!"

"No," I said. "I was looking in the window, talking to you. And then you were gone!"

"No, I was walking along, talking to Dad, and then *you* were gone!" she said. "And you scared Dad so bad!"

"I did?"

"Yes, but you didn't scare me! I always knew you were OK. I mean, who'd want to steal you? You were just being a pain, same as always!"

"Well, I had a really good time," I told her. "So ha ha! I walked *down* the Up escalator."

"Did you hear that, Dad?" the Great One said. "Did you hear what he did? He walked *down* the Up escalator. And do you know how many times Mom's told him that's dangerous?"

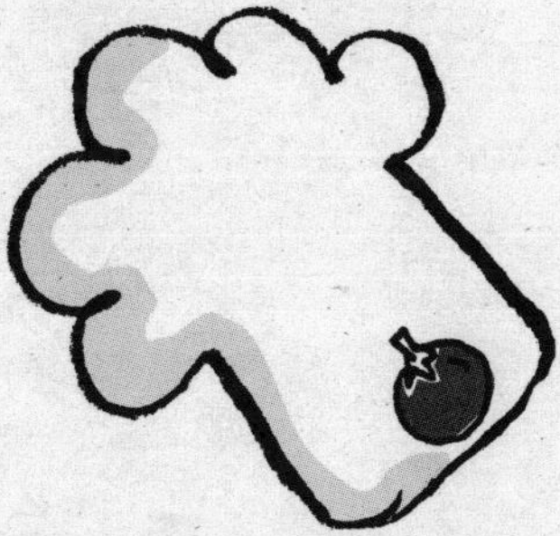

"Abigail . . ." Dad said, taking the Great One's hand. "Jake . . ." he said, taking mine. "Let's just be glad we're all together. Now, how about lunch?"

"Lunch is on the house!" the manager of the pizza place called.

"That's very nice of you," Dad said, "but not necessary."

"I insist," the manager said.

Everyone at the food court cheered.

Then the Great One said, "I'll see that robot movie if you still want to."

And I knew she was glad she found me.

Say, "Cheese!"

The Great One

We're going to visit Grandpa Pete for his birthday. Fluzzy can't come, so Charlie, our babysitter, is going to watch him. "Goodbye, Fluzzy," I said. But Fluzzy wouldn't look at me. He knew we were going away and leaving him behind. I always feel sad when I have to say goodbye

to Fluzzy. I wish I could pack him in my suitcase.

Grandpa Pete lives in Florida. Not the Disney World part of Florida. Not the beach part either. He lives in Everglades City. It's the-middle-of-nowhere, Florida. He never comes to visit us because he won't leave his birds. They're not really *his* birds, but that's what he calls them. Every morning and every night Grandpa Pete hangs his binoculars around his neck and goes out in his canoe to watch them. He knows his birds the way Mom and Dad know me and the Pain.

"Maybe we'll see an alligator this time!" the Pain sang. "Maybe we'll see a snake!" The Pain has a book, *Wildlife of the Florida Everglades*. He likes to look at the pictures.

"I don't want to see a snake," I told him.

"One time Justin had a birthday party,"

the Pain said, "and Reggie Reptile came with his snakes. One of them was a boa constrictor. That was so cool!"

"I don't want to hear any more about snakes!" I shouted.

The Pain laughed.

I decided to wear my cowboy boots on the plane.

"You don't need boots in Florida," Mom said when she saw me.

"Snakes can't bite through leather," I told her.

"Where did you hear that?" she asked.

"I read it in the Pain's book."

Mom shook her head, but she didn't say I couldn't wear my boots.

When we got to Grandpa Pete's he acted like he saw us yesterday, even though it's been a year. He's not the huggy kind of grandpa. He never says how much we've grown or how glad he is to see us.

"I've got something for you," Grandpa Pete said, holding out two cameras. "Throwaways. You each get twenty-four pictures."

"You mean it's not a digital?" the Pain asked.

"Digital?" Grandpa Pete said, as if he'd never heard the word. "This camera uses film, Jacob." Grandpa Pete never calls the Pain Jake – only Jacob. "When you've taken all your pictures the film gets developed into photos. So take your pictures carefully. You can't put more film in this camera."

"Thanks, Grandpa Pete!" I said.

I elbowed the Pain. "Oh, thanks," he said to Grandpa. He was already snapping pictures.

"*Say 'cheese!'*" he said to Dad. He got him unpacking his underwear.

"*Say 'cheese!'*" he said to Mom. He got her yawning.

"*Say 'cheese!'*" he said to Grandpa Pete.

He caught him scratching his belly.

"You're going to be sorry," I told him. "You've only got twenty-four pictures."

"So?" he said.

"So, we're going to be here three days. And when you run out, don't ask if you canuse my camera, because the answer is *no*!"

"Did I say I want to use your camera?"

"I'm just telling you the rules."

"*Say 'cheese!'*"

He snapped a picture of me with my mouth open.

"And stop taking my picture!" I told him.

He laughed.

As soon as it was dark, we went to sleep on blow-up mattresses. Grandpa Pete doesn't have a TV. He doesn't have a computer or a cellphone either. His house is just a big screened porch with one small inside room. The screens keep out most of the bugs. There are plenty of bugs. Too many for Mom. She's always swatting at something.

Early the next morning, before the sun came up, Grandpa Pete woke the Pain and me. "Shhhh . . ." he whispered, because Mom and Dad were sound asleep. We got into our long pants, long-sleeve shirts and floppy hats. We grabbed our cameras. Outside, Grandpa Pete looked down at my cowboy boots.

"You can't wear those in a canoe," he told me.

"But I have to," I said.

"They'll get wet."

"That's OK," I told him. "I don't mind."

"She's afraid of snakes," the Pain told Grandpa Pete. "She thinks they can't bite her if she's wearing boots."

"I always thought it was alligators that couldn't bite through leather," Grandpa Pete said.

Alligators too? That made me feel even better about wearing my boots!

Grandpa Pete sprayed us with citronella to keep away the mosquitoes. Then we headed for his old Jeep.

Miss Memory was waiting for us. Miss Memory is Grandpa Pete's best friend. No kidding – that's her real name. Memory Clark. She lives next door.

Grandpa Pete said, "I don't have to worry about forgetting things because I've always got my Memory with me." He makes the same joke every time we visit.

The Pain doesn't get it. He says he does, but I can tell he doesn't.

Miss Memory is a birder too. A birder is someone who watches birds. There are more than 350 kinds of birds in the Everglades, and I think Grandpa Pete and Miss Memory know them all.

The Pain got into Grandpa Pete's canoe and I went with Miss Memory. Grandpa Pete has rules for canoeing in the Everglades. Rule number one is look and listen. If we see something interesting, we can point at it, but we can't call out. That's the hardest rule for the Pain. He has no self-control. But he knows Grandpa Pete will leave him behind if he can't keep quiet. And then he'll never get to see an alligator in the wild.

Canoeing in the Everglades is like being on another planet. It's so quiet. Everywhere you look it's just water, little islands full of birds, and us. No other people. Just the *lap, lap, lap* of our canoes paddling along.

Click. I snapped a picture of a pink and white bird with a beak that looked like a spoon.

Click. I got a shot of a really big turtle.

Click. I got an osprey flying overhead.

Click. I got Grandpa Pete and the Pain in their canoe.

So far, no snakes. And no alligators either. I can't decide if I want to see an alligator or not. Suppose I see one and get so scared I scream? Suppose the alligator swims under our canoe and tips it over? Then what?

★

We went out in the canoes twice a day, early in the morning and just before sunset. On our last day Miss Memory invited me over to keep her company while she baked a pineapple upside-down cake. "It's your grandpa's favourite," she said.

"My favourite is chocolate," I told her.

"If you come back for your birthday, I'll bake you a chocolate cake."

"That's really nice, but my birthday is July fourth." I didn't want to hurt her feelings. I didn't want to say we have a party every year and all the relatives come, except Grandpa Pete – even though he's invited.

Later Miss Memory said to Mom and Dad, "I wish you'd stay longer. Three days is nothing."

"I'd say it's just about the right amount of time," Grandpa Pete said. "Any longer and they'd be bored. Or I might get sick of them."

"Pete!" Miss Memory said. "They don't know you're kidding."

"Who's kidding?" Grandpa Pete said.

I couldn't tell if he was or if he wasn't.

"I want to stay until I see an alligator," the Pain said.

"Why don't we just take them to Gatorama on the way to the airport tomorrow?" Mom suggested.

Grandpa Pete gave Mom a look. "That's for tourists," he said. "It's the real deal or nothing for my grandchildren."

Mom grew up in the city. What does she know about alligators?

Just before supper we went out in the canoes again. I must have been hungry, because I was thinking about Miss Memory's pineapple upside-down cake and wondering if I'd like it. I like cake and I like pineapple. But I've never tried them together upside-down.

Suddenly I had a creepy feeling. It wasn't just the quiet or the grey sky. I felt prickles on the back of my neck. I sat up straight, the way Fluzzy does when he knows something is going to happen. And then I saw them. In the distance. First it was just their snouts. Then they lifted their heads. Alligators!

I looked over at the Pain. But I could tell he and Grandpa Pete didn't see them yet. If they did, they'd be pointing. I turned my head to look at Miss

Memory, but she was paddling along same as always. I was the only one who saw them. Just me. They were my secret! I picked up my camera. *Say "cheese"*, I told them inside my head.

I was already thinking of how I would tell Ms Valdez, my science teacher, about seeing four alligators. *Right in front of us,* I'd say. *Close enough to touch.* That wasn't true, but it made a better story. I was so glad I was wearing my leather cowboy boots.

But how would I feel if the Pain saw alligators and didn't tell me? Not that the Pain has ever kept a secret in his entire life. But still, it would be so unfair. So I pointed. Miss Memory stopped paddling and pointed too. Then Grandpa Pete tapped the Pain on his shoulder and pointed. The Pain clapped his hand over his mouth. He was so excited he started rocking the canoe. If he fell in and got eaten by an alligator,

Mom and Dad would be really mad at Grandpa Pete.

Two of the alligators crawled up on to one of the small islands. My hands shook as I snapped pictures of them. After a minute Miss Memory started paddling backwards, very slowly, very quietly. Grandpa Pete did the same. The alligators didn't see us. At least, I don't think they did.

When we got back to the house, the Pain started yelling, "Alligators! We saw alligators."

"I hope you weren't close to them," Mom said.

"Close enough to touch!" the Pain sang. When he saw the looks on Mom's and Dad's faces he laughed. "Ha ha . . . fooled you, didn't I?"

"So you didn't see alligators?" Dad asked.

"We did!" I told Dad. "Four of them. We took pictures."

"Really, Pete," Mom said to Grandpa. "I hope you were thinking about their safety."

"I always think about the alligators' safety," Grandpa Pete said.

The next day we flew home. Fluzzy pretended not to care we were back. He had that *I don't even see you!* look on his face. But he couldn't fool me. I knew he'd missed us.

When I got into bed Mom came in, holding up my boots. "I don't think we're ever going to dry these out." She sniffed inside them and made a face. I already knew they smelled terrible, like the muck we walked through every time we went in the canoes. But I was hoping Mom would know what to do.

"We're going to have to throw them away," she said. "They're ruined."

"But I love those boots!" I cried.

"Well, Abigail . . ." She didn't say anything else. She just carried them out of my room.

"Can I get another pair?" I called.

"We'll see."

That probably meant no.

★

The next day Dad dropped off our films to be developed. He came home with the pictures that night. I couldn't wait to see how mine turned out. I knew they would be good. I knew they'd be way better than the Pain's. I opened the envelope. I took out the pictures. *What?* I thought as I flipped through half of them. "These can't be my pictures!" I cried. They were so blurry you couldn't make out anything. I grabbed the Pain's envelope. "Let me see those . . ."

"Hey!" he said. And before I could stop him he grabbed *my* envelope.

He checked out my pictures while I checked out his. But these couldn't be mine either. They were all black. "You had your finger over the lens," I told the Pain.

"Not every time," he said. "Look at this one!" He held it up. It was a perfect picture of an alligator. "Only our alligators came out right," he said.

But only *my* alligator looked like he was saying "cheese".

Fluzzy in Charge

See if I care if they go away.

See if I care if they leave me home with the babysitter.

I'll show them how much I care!

As soon as they're gone I race into *his* room.

His elephant is gone!

He took his elephant with him but not me?

See if I care!

Next I tear down the hall to *her* room.

I jump on to her bed and sniff everything.

I bite her troll doll.

I pull at its hair.

Then I knock it to the floor and hide it under the bed.

When I get thirsty I slurp from the toilet bowl.

The babysitter says,

Fluzzy, that's disgusting!

You have your own water dish.

See if I care what the babysitter says!

I hide in the mom's closet.
Way in back, behind the coats.
The babysitter can't find me.

She calls, *Fluzzy, where are you?*
Fluzzy, what am I going to tell them if you get lost?

How can I get lost when she won't let me out of the house?

When she finally opens the closet door I jump out and hiss at her.

See if I care how loud she screams!

At night I chase toy mice.

I skid across the floor.
Then back again.

She calls, *Fluzzy, you're driving me crazy!*

See if I care!

In the morning I fly down the stairs and leap on to the kitchen counter.

I paw at everything until spices fall over.

Jelly beans tumble to the floor.
Sugar spills from the bowl.
It crunches when I walk in it, like snow.

Fluzzy! she cries when she sees the mess.
Let's get this straight:
I'm in charge!

Ha ha! That's what *they* think too!

You don't want me to tell them you're a bad kitty, do you? she asks.

A bad kitty? Me?
They'd never believe that!

They might not come back if they think you're a bad kitty, she says.

But she can't scare me.

They always come back.

And when they do, I'll pretend I didn't even know they were gone.

Ben Is My Fiend

The Pain

Today at school my teacher, Mary, called my group to the reading circle. Everyone else read at their tables or in the book corner. Mary said, "Justin, will you start?" When we go to the reading circle we read from a special book called *People and Pets*. Justin read a story about a dog named Goldie.

Then Lila read about a cat called Sammy. Sammy the cat wasn't anything like my cat.

"I could write a better story about Fluzzy," I told Mary.

Mary said, "I'd like to see that story, Jake." Then she asked me to read. Just as I was about to start, another teacher came into our room and whispered something to Mary. "I have to step into the hall for a minute," Mary told our group. "I'll be right back." She looked at me. "Go ahead, Jake."

"The name of this story is 'Ben'," I said. I cleared my throat twice. "*Ben is my fiend.*" Maggie laughed. I didn't know why. So I kept reading. "*I'm glad he's my fiend because . . .*"

Everyone but David laughed this time. Justin laughed so hard he fell off his chair. When he did, his chair toppled over too. That made everyone laugh harder.

"What?" I said to my group.

"*Fiend?*" Maggie said. "Ben is your *fiend*?"

My group couldn't stop laughing. Even David laughed.

Wendy, our helper teacher, came across the room. She sat in Mary's chair. "What's up?" she asked.

"He thinks . . ." Maggie started to say.

"He thinks . . ." But she was laughing so hard she couldn't finish.

So Lila finished for her. "He thinks Ben is his *fiend*."

"What's a fiend?" David asked.

I was wondering the same thing.

"Justin, pick up your chair," Wendy said. Then she looked at me. "Jake, do you know what a fiend is?"

"No," I said.

"Can anyone help us?" Wendy asked.

Justin didn't raise his hand. He just spit it out. "A fiend is a monster! A fiend is evil."

I felt my face turn hot. I felt really stupid.

"Jake," Wendy said, "look at the picture of the two boys in the story."

The boys in the picture were laughing. They looked like friends. "Now . . . why don't you start reading again," Wendy said.

"*Ben is my fiend*," I began. I meant to say *friend*. But *fiend* just slipped out.

Now my group was out of control.

"Let's settle down, please," Wendy said. She printed both words on the board. "Jake, can you find the difference between *friend* and *fiend*?"

I looked at both words. They looked almost the same. But one had an *r* and one didn't. So I said, "Oh, I get it! A *fiend* is a *friend* without the *r*."

Now my group went crazy. Wendy couldn't get them to stop. I wanted to disappear. I pictured myself walking out of class, down the hall, out the front door and all the way home. Instead I just sat there. When Maggie laughs it sounds like she's screaming. When David laughs he sounds like a seal. Justin holds his breath when he laughs. His face gets so red it looks like he's about to explode.

The rest of the class was wondering what was going on. You could hear them whispering.

Wendy clapped her hands. "OK, that's enough! Maggie, take a turn reading, please."

"Where should I start?" Maggie asked when she finally calmed down.

"Why don't you start at the beginning of the story," Wendy said.

Maggie took a big breath. Then she started to read. "*Ben is my* fiend. *I'm glad he's my* fiend *because . . .*"

But no one was listening. They were shrieking and stomping their feet. Lila held her stomach. "It hurts . . ." she cried. "It hurts to laugh so hard!"

Wendy said, "Maggie . . . the word is *friend*!" You could tell from her voice that she'd had enough.

"I know!" Maggie said.

"Then why did you say *fiend*?" Wendy asked.

"I didn't mean to . . ."

That's when Mary came back into the room. "Everything OK?" she asked Wendy, looking at us. Mary always knows when something is going on.

"Just a little mix-up," Wendy explained, giving Mary back her chair.

Later, in the playground, my class made a circle like when we were in kindergarten. But instead of "Duck, duck, goose", Lila called, "Friend, friend, fiend!" She tapped *me* for *fiend*. I had to run around the circle trying to catch her. It didn't feel good. It didn't feel funny. Then everyone did it. Even Justin. And he's supposed to be my best friend. That was the worst.

★

At dinner the Great One looked at me and said, "What's wrong?"

"Who says anything's wrong?"

"I can tell."

Mom said, "Is something wrong, Jake?"

"I made a mistake in reading group." I pushed my pasta around on my plate.

"Everyone makes mistakes," Mom said.

"Not *this* mistake."

"I'm sure it wasn't that bad," Dad said.

"Oh yes, it was!" I told him.

Mom, Dad and the Great One waited for me to tell them more. But I didn't. The Great One started guessing. "Did you say a bad word? Is that it?"

"No."

"Did you leave out a word?"

"No."

"Did you mix up two words?"

"Maybe," I said. How did she know that was it?

"Everyone does that," she said. "It's no big deal."

But it was a big deal to me.

The next day at school when Maggie saw me she said, "Hi, *fiend*!" Everyone laughed.

In the playground I didn't play any

games. I climbed to the top of the monkey bars and stayed there.

"Help . . . *fiend*!" Victor called, pointing to me.

Everyone laughed again.

The next day at morning meeting, Mary asked if I could give the weather report. I shook my head, even though I knew the weather. So Justin got to be weather reporter instead. And Dylan got to ask the riddle of the day. "When is it dangerous to play cards?"

I knew the answer, but I wouldn't raise my hand. I was never raising my hand again. So Mary called on Marco. He said, "When the joker is wild."

Everyone clapped for Dylan's riddle and Marco's answer.

Later, Mary sat next to me during reading time. She said, "What are you reading, Jake?"

I showed her the book. *Reptiles Around the World.*

"You want to read just to me?" she asked.

I shook my head.

"You want to keep reading to yourself?"

I nodded.

"OK," Mary said.

I didn't tell her I was never reading out loud again.

★

On the school bus going home I sat next to Justin. But I didn't talk. I faced away from him and looked out the window. So Justin joked around with Dylan, who sat behind him. When we got off the bus Justin said, "Guess what I'm going to be for Halloween?"

"What?" I said.

"A *fiend*! Isn't that the best idea?"

I didn't answer. I ran the rest of the way home. I could hear Justin calling, "Jake – wait for me! Jake –" But I didn't wait.

At home I got a big piece of paper and wrote: Justin is a fiend.

That night, when Mom finished reading to me, I said, "Justin's going to be a *fiend* for Halloween."

"What are you going to be?" she asked.

"Nothing. I'm not going trick-or-treating."

Mom looked at me. "OK, but if you

change your mind, I'll help with your costume."

"I'm not wearing a costume."

Mom kissed me goodnight. When she was gone, I got out of bed and tiptoed to my closet. I reached up and grabbed my Wolfman mask. Grandma bought it for me over the summer. It's pretty scary. I pulled it on. "What do you think, Fluzzy? Do I look like a fiend?" Fluzzy yawned. What does he care about fiends? Then I yanked off the mask and got back into bed.

Bruno was waiting for me. *Bruno* is my best friend now.

★

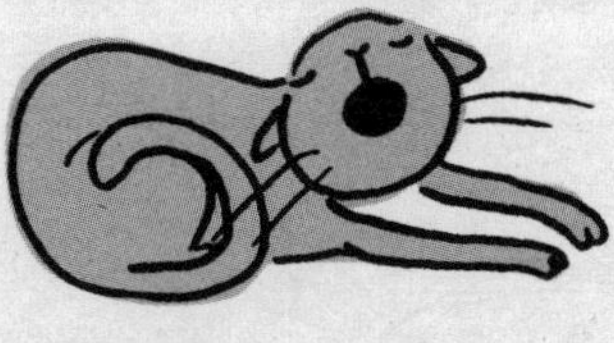

On Halloween night the Great One danced into the living room. She was wearing a tutu, cowboy boots and a red wig. She carried a magnifying glass. "How do you like it?" she asked.

"What are you supposed to be?"

"You can't tell?"

I didn't answer.

She sighed. "I guess you're just not old enough to know."

"Know what?"

"Spy Dancer."

"Who's Spy Dancer?"

"Never mind!" She turned and twirled to the front door. She was going trick-or-treating with her friends.

"We could go trick-or-treating too," Dad said to me.

"I'm not going trick-or-treating." I put on my Wolfman mask, and every time the bell rang I opened the door. A couple of little kids screamed when they saw me. One girl said, "What are you supposed to be?"

"A fiend," I told her.

"What's a fiend?"

"It's the opposite of a friend."

"Oh," she said, reaching into the candy bowl. She helped herself to three mini-boxes of raisins. At least I think that's what they were. It's not that easy to see when you're wearing a Wolfman mask.

The next time the bell rang it was Justin. I saw his dad waiting for him on the sidewalk. He was wearing a monster mask, but I recognized him anyway. Last year we went trick-or-treating together.

"Are you supposed to be what I think you're supposed to be?" he asked.

"Yes," I told him. And I growled. He growled too and took a handful of candy from the bowl.

Then we just stood there looking at each other through the eyeholes in our monster masks. Finally Justin said, "I have an idea."

I said, "Me too."

"You go first," Justin said.

"No, you go first."

"OK," Justin said. "Remember

last year when we went trick-or-treating together?"

I nodded.

"We could do that again."

I pretended to think it over. Then I said, "Deal."

I found Dad and told him I'd changed my mind. I was going trick-or-treating after all. Dad helped me into my jacket and gave me a loot bag.

"Ready?" Justin asked when I came back.

"Ready," I said.

We jumped off the porch and ran down the street together.

Later, when I got home, I ate two Crunch bars from my loot bag. Then I added an *r* to the sign that said *Justin is a fiend!*

Useless

The Great One

We're going to Uncle Phil's apartment in New York. You have to drive through a tunnel to get there. Either that or drive over a bridge. But the tunnel is faster for us. The Pain doesn't like tunnels. "Tell me when . . ." he kept saying to Mom.

As we came up to the entrance of the tunnel Mom said, "OK . . . now."

And the Pain slid to the floor of the back seat of our car. He covered his eyes

with his hands. "Tell me when we're out."

"You are beyond hopeless," I told him.

"Abigail . . ." Mom warned.

"It's just a road," I argued.

"An underwater road," the Pain said from the floor.

"And he's not in his seat belt," I added.

"Thank you, Abigail," Mom said.

"Thank you for what?" I asked.

I could hear Mom sigh.

"You'd better not get carsick while you're down there," I said to the Pain.

"I'm not carsick," the Pain said.

"Because puking in the car isn't allowed," I told him.

"Abigail . . ." Mom said. "Stop talking about it or you'll make him sick."

"Me? Make him carsick? Why would I want to do that?"

"That's enough, Abigail," Mom said.

As we came out of the tunnel Mom called to the Pain, "All clear!" And the Pain sat in his seat again and fastened his seat belt.

"Invisible line," I reminded him. *Invisible line* is how we divide the back seat of the car. I have my side and he has his. But he gave me a kick anyway.

So I gave him one back.

"Children," Mom said, "Dad can't concentrate on the road when you're acting up."

We got to Uncle Phil's apartment in time for lunch. But there was no sign of food. Our cousins William and Sierra were there.

William is twelve and Sierra is fifteen. Last time we saw them was before Uncle Phil got divorced and moved to New York. When Mom asked if she could help get lunch ready, Uncle Phil looked surprised. He tore off the top of a paper bag and scribbled a shopping list on it. Then he gave Sierra some money and told her and William to go to the big deli on the corner.

William pointed at the Pain and me. "What are *they* . . . useless?"

Before I could say anything,

before I could tell him *Useless is as useless does* or something like that, Sierra laughed. "Yeah," she said. "They can help us carry everything home."

I didn't want to go anywhere with William and Sierra.

"Jake and Abigail don't know their way around New York," Mom said.

"You think *we* do?" Sierra said. "This is the first time we're visiting our dad since he moved here."

"Why don't I come with you?" Mom said.

"If *you're* going, you don't need William and me," Sierra said to Mom. "Besides, I have a lot to do."

"Like what?" William asked.

"None of your business," Sierra told him.

"*None of your business,*" William sang, mocking his sister.

Sierra looked like she wanted to slug him.

The Pain looked at me. I knew what he was thinking – William and Sierra are worse than us. Much worse.

"You kids are going," Uncle Phil told William and Sierra, "and that's that!"

"Fine," Sierra said. And she grabbed the list out of Uncle Phil's hand.

Mom said, "Abigail and Jake will come with us. That will give Uncle Phil and Dad some time alone."

Why would Dad want to be alone with Uncle Phil? I wondered. Uncle Phil isn't a fun uncle. He's nothing like Uncle Mitch. Mitch taught me to ride my bike. I don't think Uncle Phil likes kids. I'm not sure he likes anyone, not even William and Sierra. He and Dad are complete opposites. I don't see how they can be brothers.

★

The deli was huge. It took up a whole block. It was busy too. There were lines everywhere. Mom took charge. "William, get on the bread line."

"Do I have to?"

"Yes," Mom said, "if you ever want to have lunch." Then she told Sierra to get a number and wait on line at the deli meats counter.

"No way," Sierra said. "I'm a veggie. I don't go near that stuff."

"OK . . ." Mom said. "You can pick up the cheese and the rest of what's on the list. I'll wait on line here."

"*She* has to help me," Sierra said, pointing at me.

"My name is Abigail," I told her.

"Whatever," Sierra said.

Sierra used to be nice. One time when I was little we baked cupcakes together.

I followed her through the deli. "I hate this city," she said, loud enough for anyone to hear. A couple of people turned to look at her. "You can't ride your horse or anything."

"You have a horse?" I asked.

Sierra said, "We have six horses. You probably don't know, but we moved to Montana with our mom. You probably don't even know where Montana is."

"Yes, I do," I told her. I tried to picture the map of the states on the wall in my classroom. Montana . . . Montana . . . which state was Montana?

"It's out west," Sierra told me.

"I know that," I said.

"I ride my horse to school."

"That sounds so cool."

"You know what's not cool?" she asked.

"What?"

"You and your family. And that includes my dad."

"That's rude," I told her.

She laughed and shoved the list in my face. "Get this stuff. I've got to text my boyfriend." She pushed a basket at me, then took off.

I didn't know what to get. I mean, I could read the list, but there were about fifty kinds of mustard on the shelf. I threw in the one with the fanciest label. Next on the list was olive oil. There were rows and rows of olive oil. I chose the one in the prettiest bottle. But what kind of cheese was I supposed to get? I stood in front of the cheese counter. There were so many! A hundred, at least. I didn't recognize any of the names.

"Do you need some help?" a woman asked.

"I need cheese," I told her.

"What kind?"

"I don't know. For lunch."

"How about Cheddar?" she said.

"Is it white? My brother only eats white food."

She reached for a chunk of cheese and handed it to me. "I think this will do the trick," she said.

I thanked her, then looked around for Sierra. I didn't see her anywhere, so I ran through the store looking for Mom. I kept going down the wrong aisles. Once I passed William. "Hey," he called. "Cousin . . ." Like he couldn't remember my name.

Finally I found Mom and the Pain. Mom was still waiting for her number to be called. "Where's Sierra?" she asked.

I shrugged.

"Why didn't you stay with her?"

I shrugged again.

Mom took my basket. "I didn't know which kind of mustard to get . . . or olive oil . . . or cheese . . ."

"You did a good job," Mom said.

"Did you get something for me?" the Pain asked.

"White cheese," I told him.

He nodded. "Good."

When all our shopping was done Mom

found Sierra outside the store, yakking on her cellphone. Mom handed each of us a bag to carry, and she carried two.

We were almost back at Uncle Phil's when I tripped on the kerb and fell. The bag I was carrying flew out of my hand. Lemons rolled down the sidewalk, packages of deli meat flew out and a bag of sandwich rolls landed with a thud.

"Oh, honey . . ." Mom said, helping me up. "Are you OK?"

I looked down at my knees. They were scraped and bloody and one of them had pebbles stuck to it. I definitely wasn't OK.

"Jake," Mom called, "get those lemons! William, pick up the rolls and the deli meats."

Sierra shook her head. "Useless . . ." she said, looking at my knees.

"Really, Sierra . . ." Mom said. "Surely you can be kinder than that."

DON'T
WALK
TAXI
hotdogs
Best in
NYC
TAXI

"I don't think so," Sierra muttered.

Mom handed Sierra money and asked her to go to the closest pharmacy. "We need antiseptic and Band-Aids," Mom told her. "Unless your dad has them at the apartment."

"How would I know?" Sierra said.

"Let's not take a chance," Mom said. "Just go and get them. There's a pharmacy on almost every block. Then come back to the apartment."

"You expect a lot," Sierra told Mom.

Mom muttered something to herself.

While the Pain chased lemons, William opened the package of sandwich rolls and shoved one in his mouth.

"William . . ." Mom said.

"I'm hungry," William told her.

"We're all hungry," Mom said.

"And some of us are injured," I added, in case he didn't know. Blood trickled down one of my legs, and my knees burned like crazy.

When we got back to the apartment, Dad met us at the door. Mom shoved the shopping bags at him and said, "Don't ask . . ." Then she took me to the bathroom and washed my knees.

"Ouch . . ." I kept saying. But when Sierra got back with the alcohol they burned even worse. Mom kept saying she was sorry but she had to make sure they were clean.

At last we sat down to lunch. Dad was the only one still in a good mood. He tried to get Sierra and William to talk. He asked them questions about school. They didn't answer. He tried riddles, but only the Pain laughed at the answers.

Then he tried to get Uncle Phil to talk about when they were growing up. That was a big mistake.

"Let me tell you what it was like back then," Uncle Phil said to the rest of us, and I didn't like the way he smiled. "Little Andy could do no wrong." Andy is Dad's name. "Little Andy was everyone's favourite. Just ask him."

"Come on, Phil. . . ." Dad said. "We're grown-ups now . . . it's time to let that go."

But Sierra jumped in. "I know just how you feel, Dad," she said, "because William is the favourite in *our* family and I'm less than zero. Isn't that right?"

"I like being the favourite," William said.

"I'm sure I'd like being the favourite too," Sierra said.

The Pain looked over at me.

"What are you kids talking about?" Uncle Phil finally asked. "I don't play favourites."

It got really quiet. So I said, "Did you know Sierra rides her horse to school in Montana? Isn't that cool?"

William snorted. He sounded like a horse.

"Montana?" Uncle Phil said. Then his voice boomed. "Her horse?"

"She has six horses." I knew I should stop, but I couldn't help myself.

"Six horses?" Uncle Phil repeated.

Sierra shouted, "Yes, six horses! That's how it could be if you and Mom—"

Uncle Phil didn't wait for her to finish. "That's enough, Sierra!" Sierra's face turned red. She shoved back her chair and ran for the bathroom. The door slammed.

"This is a fun lunch," William said.

That's when the Pain spilled his milk all over William. "Useless!" William shouted at him. "Look at this . . . I'm soaked."

Mom jumped up to get kitchen towels. I could tell the Pain wanted to cry. He got out of his seat, went over to Dad and rested his head against Dad's shoulder. "Can we go now?" he whispered.

"Soon," Dad said. Then he looked at Uncle Phil. "Phil, I think—"

"I don't give a hooey what you think, Andy! So keep it to yourself for once."

We left Uncle Phil's right after lunch. Dad was really upset. Usually nothing bothers him, but this time was different. "My brother and those kids . . ." he said so quietly I could hardly hear him.

"They're teenagers," Mom reminded him. "They're going through a lot."

"Don't worry, Dad," I said. "We're

never going to be like William and Sierra. Right, Jake?"

"They're *fiends*," the Pain said.

"They behaved badly," Mom said. "I won't argue with that."

"They called us *useless*!" I said.

"The divorce has been hard on them," Mom said.

"They have their own horses," I said.

Mom and Dad looked at each other. "Sierra probably wishes they had horses," Mom said.

"You mean she doesn't have her own horse?"

Dad shook his head.

"But how do you know? They live in Montana."

Mom and Dad looked at each other again. "Actually they live in Cincinnati," Mom said.

"Is that in Montana?" I asked.

"No, it's a city in Ohio," Dad said.

"You mean Sierra was lying?" I asked.

"Sometimes there's a fine line between lying and wishing," Mom said.

"That's just a nice way to say she was lying," I said. And then I remembered the time I told my friends I could ride a bike when I couldn't. Did that mean I was like Sierra?

"Where's Ohio?" the Pain asked.

"When we get home I'll show you on a map," Dad said.

Mom looked around. "It's such a beautiful day. It's a shame to waste it. How about a quick trip to the zoo in Central Park?"

Mom always comes up with good ideas. So we went to the zoo and watched the penguins. And all the way home the Pain and I were really nice to each other, even going through the tunnel.

DO NOT
FEED
THE PENGUINS

When we got home Dad spread out the atlas on the floor. An atlas is a big book of maps. Dad's is very old. He got it when he graduated from high school. He showed us Cincinnati on the map of Ohio.

The Pain said, "I'm glad Sierra's not my sister."

And I said, "I'm glad William's not my brother."

Then we both jumped on Dad.

"And we're really, really glad Uncle Phil's not our dad."

Dad hugged us and said, "And I'm really glad you two are my kids."

She Stole My Story

The Great One

I told Sasha about Sunday at Uncle Phil's. I told her how William and Sierra called us *useless*. Then I made her promise never to tell anyone, not even Emily or Kaylee.

That afternoon our teacher, Mr Gee, said, "Today we're going to write a story in class."

"Is it a *never take your pencil off the paper* story?" Lucas asked.

"Yes," Mr Gee said. "From the time I

say *go* to the time I say *stop,* just write, write, write."

"About what?" Emily asked.

"Something that happened to you," Mr Gee said. "This time let's make it about something you didn't like."

When Mr Gee said, "Go!" I started writing. I wrote about the time we visited a farm and a goose chased me. He honked and snapped at my behind. I screamed until Dad rescued me.

I kept writing, writing, writing until Mr Gee called, "Pencils down!" Then he asked who would like to read their story to the class. Half the class raised their hands, including me. Mr Gee called on Sasha.

Sasha went to the front of the room. "The name of my story is 'Useless', " she said.

I looked up.

Then she started to read. And the story she started to read was *my* story – the story I'd told her about visiting Uncle Phil. Only she wrote it like it happened to *her* instead of to me. I couldn't believe it. I trusted her when she promised she'd never ever tell, and now she was telling the whole world. My heart started beating

really fast. I felt like grabbing her paper and ripping it to shreds.

When she finished Mr Gee said, "Good work, Sasha."

Sasha smiled.

As soon as I could, I went over to her desk. "You stole my story!"

"Not really," she said. "I just wrote about it."

"But it happened to me, not you!"

"So?"

"So, we're supposed to be friends. And friends don't steal from each other."

"I didn't think you'd mind," Sasha said. "I thought you'd like the idea."

"You what?"

"You heard me, Abigail," she said. "I thought you'd like the idea."

"Liar!" I shouted. Our class got very quiet. Everyone was listening. But I didn't care.

"You have no right to call me names," Sasha said very quietly.

"I'm never speaking to you again," I told her.

"Fine, then I'm never speaking to you either."

"I said it first," I told her.

"I *thought* it first," she said.

"You copy everything," I told her. "Even my thoughts!"

"Copying is the highest form of flattery," she said.

"Who told you that?" I asked.

"My mother," she said.

"Then maybe your mother is a copycat too. Maybe your mother steals from her friends, just like you!"

"Abigail!" Mr Gee said sharply. "Sasha!"

I went up to Mr Gee. But before I could say *She stole my story,* the bell rang and the school day was over.

I didn't sit near Sasha on the bus going home. I sat with Emily. I told her the whole story. "No wonder you're mad," she said.

That night, before dinner, Mom asked if I was feeling OK. "I hate Sasha!" I said.

"But Sasha's your friend," Mom said.

"*Was* my friend."

Mom took the chicken out of the oven. "Want to talk about it?"

So while she was dishing out the green beans and potatoes I told her how Sasha stole my story.

"That must have hurt," Mom said.

"It did. It hurt really bad."

Telling Mom made me feel better. So at dinner I told Dad how Sasha stole my story. "She wrote it exactly the way I told it to her."

"Did she write about me?" the Pain asked.

"Not every story is about you," I said.

Then I went on and on. "She even wrote about my knees." I stopped for a minute, to check them. They didn't have scabs yet.

"I wanted to rip the paper out of her hand and tear it into teeny tiny bits."

"You should have," the Pain said.

Before we went to bed the Pain asked, "How do you spell *Sasha*?"

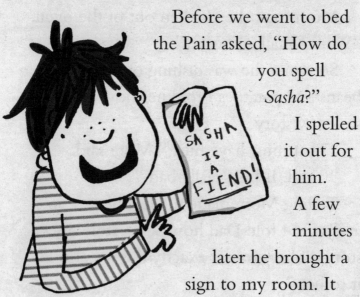

I spelled it out for him.

A few minutes later he brought a sign to my room. It

said: *Sasha is a Fiend!* He helped me tape it to the wall above my bed. "Thank you," I said.

The Pain smiled.

The next morning on the school bus I didn't look at Sasha. She didn't look at me either. It was the same in class. And in the playground.

That afternoon Mr Gee called us up to his desk. Before he even asked what was going on, I blurted it out. "That story Sasha read yesterday . . . she stole it from me."

"My mother says copying is the highest form of flattery," Sasha repeated.

Mr Gee looked at Sasha, then he looked at me. "I hope you two can work this out on your own," he said.

Madison Purdy got all the girls in our class to choose sides. She made it me against Sasha. I can't stand Madison Purdy. One time at ballet she called me a weed. Now she acted like she was in charge of the whole world. Emily sided with me. Kaylee sided with Sasha. My stomach hurt almost all the time.

On Friday Mr Gee called Sasha and me up to his desk again. "This has gone far enough."

"But . . ." I started to say.

"No *buts*," Mr Gee said.

"*If only* Madison . . ." Sasha began, but Mr Gee stopped her, too.

"No *if onlys*."

"Give us one more chance," Sasha said.

"OK," Mr Gee said. "But this is it."

In the playground my group huddled to one side and Sasha's group huddled to the other. Everybody had ideas of what we should do. But we couldn't agree on anything. Finally Sasha and Kaylee came over to us. The other girls backed away until it was just me and Emily and Kaylee and Sasha. Kaylee said, "Sasha has something to say to you, Abigail." She gave Sasha a little nudge.

"I'm sorry I used your story," Sasha said.

"You mean *stole* my story," I said.

SCHOOL
3

"She didn't steal it," Kaylee said. "She borrowed it."

Emily said, "You can't borrow something if you don't ask first."

"I never thought of that," Kaylee said. She looked at Sasha. "Emily's right. It's like you can't borrow my jacket unless you ask and then I say OK."

Sasha was quiet for a minute. "From now on I'll ask," she said.

"And when a friend tells you something that's private you won't blab it all over town?" I said.

"I didn't blab it," Sasha said. "Nobody knew it was your family until *you* blabbed it."

That was probably true, I thought. But still . . .

Mr Gee came over to us. "How's it going?"

Now Kaylee and Emily backed away,

leaving just me and Sasha. "You want to know why I did it?" Sasha asked. "Because my family is so boring. Nothing ever happens in my family."

"Sasha," Mr Gee said, "can you understand why Abigail feels you betrayed her?"

"I guess." Sasha choked up. "But *she* dissed my mom. She said my mom steals from her friends."

"I said *maybe* your mom steals from her friends."

Mr Gee rocked back and forth on his heels.

I knew what I had to do. I just didn't want to do it. "OK," I said, and I took a big breath. "I'm sorry I dissed your mom."

"You're really sorry?" Sasha said.

"Yes."

"Good."

"Well," Mr Gee said, "I'm glad you two worked out your problems." He went over to a group of boys.

Sasha turned to me and said, "I'll tell you a secret if you promise not to tell."

"I promise."

"This was the worst week of my life. I couldn't even eat, my stomach hurt so bad."

I didn't tell her how bad *my* stomach hurt. Instead I told her about the sign over my bed, the one that says *Sasha is a fiend!* "But I'm going to take it down today."

"You really thought I was a *fiend*?"

"Actually my brother made the sign and gave it to me."

"Your brother thought I was a *fiend*?"

"Well, yes . . . because you stole my story."

"I don't see how I can be friends with someone who thought I was a fiend."

"I *said* it was my brother, not me."

"But you put the sign over your bed!"

I never should have told her about the sign. What was I thinking?

Emily and Kaylee came up to us. "So, you two are friends again, right?" Emily asked.

Sasha and I looked at each other. "Friends or fiends," Sasha said. "We haven't decided yet."

"It's better to be friends," Emily and Kaylee said at the same time. They slapped hands, spun around three times and pretended to spit.

Sasha and I started laughing. We laughed all the way back to our classroom.

Snow Day

The Pain

"Snow day!" I jumped on to the Great One's bed. "School's closed." I shook her. "Come on, wake up!"

"Mmmph . . . bafa . . ." she mumbled.

I shook her again. "Open your eyes."

She swatted at me like I was a mosquito. I grabbed her feet and started pulling. I pulled her right off the bed. She landed on the rug with a thud. But she still didn't open her eyes. So I dragged her across the floor to

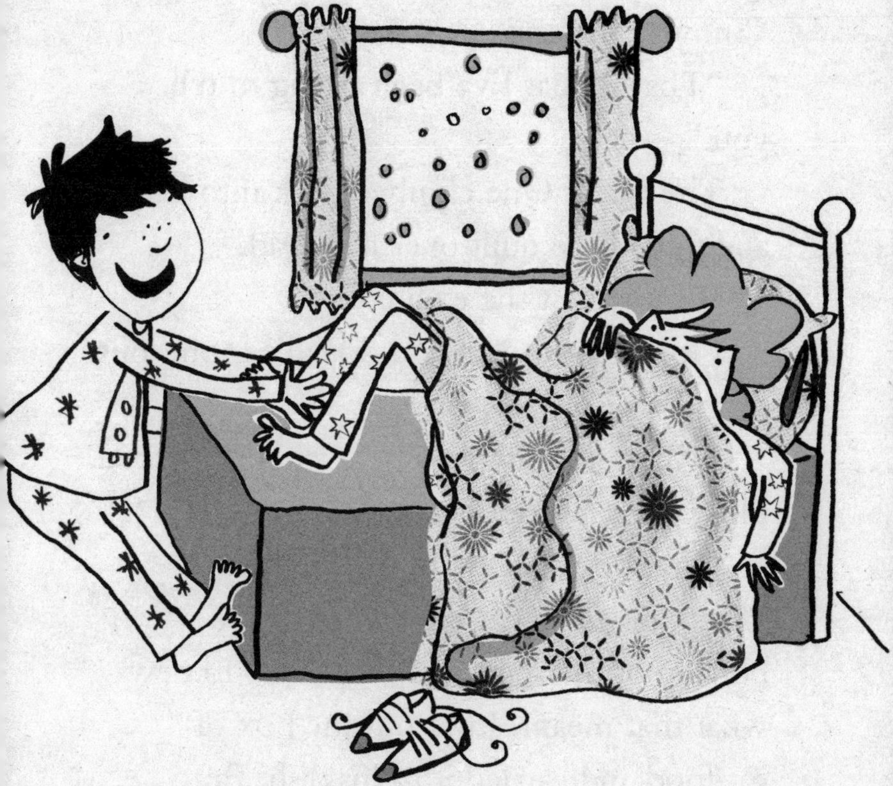

the window. This time she opened her eyes.
"Look!" I said, pointing at the window.

"This better be good." She knelt in

front of the window and looked outside. "Snow?" she said.

"That's what I've been trying to tell you."

The Great One climbed back into bed and pulled the quilt over her head.

Why wasn't she excited?

I looked into Mom and Dad's room, but they were still sleeping.

"Why isn't anyone else excited?" I asked Fluzzy. He just looked at me.

I crept downstairs to the kitchen. Fluzzy flew by me. He waited at the bottom of the stairs and miaowed. I knew what that meant. I got out the box of cat food and carried it to his dish. But before I could fill it I had to take out the three toy mice he'd stashed there. Every night, while we're sleeping, Fluzzy plays with his toy mice. We don't know why he leaves them in his food dish. I lifted them out by their tails. Fluzzy watched as I sniffed them. They smelled like the inside of his mouth.

The Great One won't touch Fluzzy's mice. She says they're disgusting. Probably that's why Fluzzy likes me best. The Great One can't stand that Fluzzy sleeps on my bed. It makes her crazy that I'm Fluzzy's favourite. Maybe if she'd sniff his mice he'd like her better.

I gave Fluzzy fresh water and poured food into his bowl.

While he chowed down I opened the front door and stuck out my head. Brrrr . . . it was freezing. But I didn't care how cold it was. I pulled my snow jacket over my pyjamas, got into my snow boots and grabbed a hat and mittens. I closed the door behind me so Fluzzy couldn't get out.

I almost slid down the front steps because the snow was so deep you couldn't tell exactly where they were. Everything was white. I jumped off the steps. The snow was fluffy. It wasn't as high as my waist, but it came up past my knees.

I clomped around the front yard. I started trying to build a fort, but it wasn't that much fun by myself. So I gave up and rolled in the snow. I rolled all the

way across our front yard. And all the way back.

By then I had snow down my neck. My pyjama bottoms were soaked. Plus I was hungry. So I went to the front door. But the doorknob wouldn't turn. I banged on it. I rang the bell ten times. I called, "Hello . . . let me in!"

Fluzzy came to the window next

to the door and looked out at me.

"Go get Mom or Dad," I told him.

He pawed at the glass, but that was all. I banged again. Louder this time.

"Hello . . . somebody . . . anybody . . ."

Finally the Great One opened the door. She looked me up and down. "Why are you wearing pyjamas in the snow?"

I didn't answer.

"You'd better change before Mom sees you."

But it was too late. Mom was already coming down the stairs. "Jake . . . you went out in the snow in your pyjamas?" she said, like she couldn't believe it. "What were you thinking?"

I wasn't thinking anything except about the snow, but I didn't tell that to Mom.

"Go upstairs and change into dry

clothes," Mom said. "And bring me those wet pyjamas."

Fluzzy smiled. Some people think cats can't smile, but I know they can. Sometimes Fluzzy laughs, even if I'm the only one who knows it.

*

We were just about finished with breakfast when Justin came to the door. “Can Jake come out to play?” he asked Dad.

“Snow fort!” we yelled when we were outside. We started building in the front yard. Dylan came over. Then a couple of other boys. Then Michael and Eric from fifth grade. We all worked together. I wished every day could be a snow day!

When the Great One’s friends came over she raced out of the house with Fluzzy right behind her.

Eric shouted, “No girls allowed in our fort!”

“Who’d want to be in your fort?” the Great One said. She and her friends laughed and went to the backyard.

Fluzzy sniffed the air. He tasted the snow. Then very slowly, he tried walking in it. I called to him, “Come on, Fluzz . . . you can do it."

That's when Madison Purdy and her little brother, Brett, showed up. What were they doing at our house? The Great One says if Madison Purdy was the last person on earth, she still wouldn't be friends with her.

Fluzzy flew over the snow to our fort. Madison Purdy stopped in her tracks when she saw him. "I know that cat."

"No, you don't," I said.

"He looks just like my cat who ran away."

"Well, he's not," I told her. "He's *my* cat."

"No, really . . ." she said. "I think it *is* Mister."

"It's not Mister," I argued. "It's Fluzzy." I wondered who would name a cat *Mister*?

"I don't care if you stole my cat," she

said. "Because Mister was stupid and mean. He was always hissing."

Fluzzy took one look at Madison Purdy, hissed and ran for his life. He ducked under the porch of our house.

Madison watched. "Didn't that cat look like Mister?" she asked Brett.

"Mister was a bad cat," Brett said. "He didn't like me."

"That's because you pulled his tail."

"I pulled his tail because he didn't like me."

"Just stay away from *my* cat," I told them both.

"Where are the girls?" Madison asked. "I heard they were over here."

"In the back," I told her.

Madison headed for the backyard, dragging Brett with her.

I went back to work on our fort with the other boys. It was a big fort. The biggest snow fort ever. But before we'd finished building it, before we'd even started making snowballs, someone yelled, "*Attack!*" and the girls came rushing at us, pounding us with snowballs.

Thwack!

Smash!

Oomph!

Ouch!

We fought back. We scooped together snowballs as fast as we could, but by then the girls were leaping over our fort, jumping on to our backs. Justin went down. Dylan went down. *Wham!* I was tackled from behind and pushed face down in the snow. I tried to yell for help. I tried to kick. But someone sat on my

legs and held my head down. I couldn't breathe. Just when I thought that might be the end of me, someone else pulled her off.

"What do you think you're doing to my brother?" It was the Great One.

"Washing his face in snow," Madison Purdy said.

"How would you feel if I washed *your* little brother's face in snow?" the Great One asked Madison.

"I wouldn't mind," Madison said. "He deserves it."

"So do you!" The Great One scooped up a handful of snow and shoved it in Madison's face.

Brett jumped up and down, clapping his hands. "Do it again!"

Madison said, "Shut up, Brett!" She grabbed his arm and pulled him away. "Let's get out of here."

"And don't come back!" the Great One shouted. "That means never!"

"Never would be too soon for me!" Madison yelled.

As they were leaving Michael yelled, "Truce!" And the snowballs stopped flying.

Then Eric shouted, "Sledding on Holden Hill!"

In two minutes all the kids were racing home to get their sleds.

The Great One ran for the garage to get hers. “This is the best day in the history of the world!” she sang. “You were right to be excited. Maybe it’ll snow again tonight. Maybe tomorrow will be another snow day.”

But I was thinking, One snow day at a time is enough for me. Fluzzy came out from under the house. I’m pretty sure he was thinking the same thing.

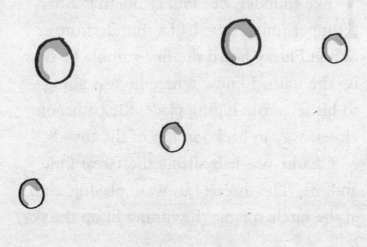

How Fluzzy Got His Name

The Pain

I like thunder, but Fluzzy doesn't. After supper tonight we had a thunderstorm. When Fluzzy heard the first rumble he flew up the stairs. I knew where he was going – to his favourite hiding place: the bathroom closet, way in back, on top of the towels.

Charlie was babysitting the Great One and me. The three of us were playing Uno at the kitchen table. Lightning lit up the sky.

Then *crash!* "That was a big one!" I shouted. I had to shout because the Great One had cotton wool stuffed in her ears. She says she's not afraid of thunder. But I don't believe her.

"What's today's date?" the Great One asked Charlie. She took the cotton wool out of one of her ears so she could hear.

Charlie checked her watch. "April twenty-eighth," she said. Charlie's watch can tell the time around the world. It tells the date too.

"April twenty-eighth," the Great One said. "I knew it!"

"Knew what?" I said.

"It's Fluzzy's birthday!"

"We don't know when Fluzzy was born," I reminded her.

"But April twenty-eighth is the day we found him," she said. "Exactly one year ago. Charlie was babysitting that night too. And it was pouring down rain just like now."

Bang! Another clap of thunder. The Great One stuck the cotton wool back in her ear. Then she called, "Uno." I knew she would win. She always wins.

“We should have a party for Fluzzy,” she said.

“Should we make hats?” I asked.

“First cupcakes,” the Great One said. “Then hats.” She jumped up from the table.

“Pointy hats or the other kind?” I asked.

“You choose.”

“Really . . . I get to choose?” The Great One hardly ever lets me choose.

Charlie followed the Great One. “I’m not much of a baker,” she said.

“Don’t worry,” the Great One said. “I know how to bake cupcakes.”

The Great One stood on a step stool at the kitchen counter and lined up everything she needed for the cupcakes.

“I only eat white cupcakes,” I reminded her. “With white frosting on top.”

“You think I don’t know that?” she said.

"I thought maybe you forgot."

"Well, I didn't."

"OK." Then I got an idea. I'd make place mats for the party. I know how to make place mats because we made them at school for restaurant day. So I got some paper and markers. I started making a picture of a dark and stormy night. I put lightning in the sky. Next I drew a small cat. He was lost and scared and wet. "Remember how we heard Fluzzy miaowing outside the kitchen door?" I asked.

"I heard him first," the Great One said. "And I ran to the kitchen door."

"No, you didn't! *I* ran to the kitchen door."

"You followed me," the Great One said.

"No, you followed me!"

Charlie said, "I think all three of us got there at the same time."

"But I *saw* him first!" the Great One said. "He was so wet and . . ."

". . . he was shaking," I added.

"I hate when you finish my sentences," the Great One said.

"Abigail," Charlie said, "are you paying attention to the recipe?"

"Yes," the Great One said.

The thunder was moving away now, but it was still raining. I made another place mat. This time I drew Mom and Dad when they saw Fluzzy for the first time. Only he wasn't Fluzzy then. He was: The Lost Cat.

When Mom and Dad got home that night they were really surprised to see a cat slurping milk from a saucer. "What's this?" Mom asked.

"This is Fluffy!" the Great One said.

"No, it's Fuzzy!" I said. "We saved him from the storm."

"But who does he belong to?" Mom asked.

"He belongs to us now," the Great One sang.

We begged Mom and Dad to let us keep him.

But Mom said, "First we'll have to find out if his owner is looking for him."

And Dad said, "In the morning we'll call the animal shelter."

"And we'll put an ad in the paper," Mom added.

"Why?" the Great One asked.

"Because that's the right thing to do," Dad said. "If you lost your pet, you'd want the person who found him to return him to you, wouldn't you?"

"I'd never let my pet get lost," she said.

We made him a bed with some old towels. He curled up, yawned and closed his eyes.

"Good night, Fluffy," the Great One said.

"Good night, Fuzzy," I said.

The two of us went upstairs to get ready for bed.

"His name is *Fluffy,*" the Great One said as we brushed our teeth.

"No, it's *Fuzzy*!" I argued. My mouth was full of toothpaste.

"Fluffy!"

"Fuzzy!"

We both dribbled toothpaste down our chins.

★

Three days went by. No one knew anything about a lost cat. Not the police. Not the animal shelter. Not the newspaper. Nobody put up a LOST CAT sign with a picture. So we took him to the vet.

The vet told us he was healthy and not even a year old. "What's his name?" she asked.

"Fuzzy," I answered.

"No, it's Fluffy!" the Great One said.

That night Fuzzy was curled up on Mom's lap, purring. She said, "If we're keeping him, it's time to decide on a name."

"I have decided," the Great One said. "It's Fluffy."

"I've decided too," I said. "And it's Fuzzy!"

Dad said, "He needs *one* name. So how

about a combination of Fluffy and Fuzzy?"

"You mean like *Fuffy*?" the Great One said. "No cat wants to be called *Fuffy*!"

"No cat wants to be called *Zuffy* either," I said.

And then all four of us started throwing out combinations.

"Yuzzy?"

"Luffy?"

"Uzzy?"

"Zyuff?

"Fyzu?"

"Fyzu," Dad said. "I kind of like that one."

"Daaad . . ." the Great One said, shaking her head. I shook mine too. No way were we calling our cat *Fyzu*. Instead, the Great One started to say, "It has to be *Fl* . . ."

And I finished with ". . . *uzzy*." We

looked at each other and laughed. Then we high-fived to seal the deal.

And that's how Fluzzy got his name.

Unicorn

The Great One

Everything was ready for Fluzzy's party. When the storm ended Fluzzy came back to the kitchen. The Pain said, "Guess what, Fluzz? You're having a party!"

"Don't tell him!" I called. "You'll spoil the surprise."

"You think he knows what *party* means?" the Pain asked.

"Stop . . ." I said. "Before you ruin everything."

"When do we put on his par . . ." the Pain started to say. Then he stopped and started again. This time he spelled it out. "When do we put his *h-a-t* on him?" he asked.

"Not yet," I said.

When we heard the front door open Charlie grabbed her backpack and umbrella. "Wish I could stay for the *you-know-what*," she said, "but I have a class at college tonight."

As Mom and Dad came into the kitchen I yelled, "Surprise!"

"Are we celebrating something?" Dad asked Mom. "Did I forget our anniversary?"

Mom laughed. "Our anniversary is in June."

"Then what?" Dad said.

"We're celebrating Fluzzy's birthday!" The Pain danced around like he always

does when he's excited. "He came to live with us one year ago. April twenty-eighth. Remember?"

"It was *my* idea," I told Mom and Dad. "*I'm* the one who remembered."

"What a good memory you have, Abigail," Mom said.

"I have a good memory too," the Pain said.

"But not as good as mine," I argued. "I have the best memory in the family. Just ask Grandma. She's always saying so."

"I remember that night," Dad said. "It was raining even harder than tonight."

I cooed at Fluzzy. "And you were just a lost wet kitty, weren't you?" Fluzzy miaowed. I handed party hats to Mom and Dad. They put them on. I tried to get Fluzzy to wear his too. But he kept shaking it off, then biting it. "Stop that, Fluzzy," I said.

The Pain laughed.

Dad got his camera. After a couple of pictures Mom started sniffing. "Is something in the oven?" she asked.

"Oh no. . . ." I ran for the oven, with Mom right behind me. She grabbed the oven gloves and lifted out the tray of cupcakes. But

it was too late. "They're ruined!" I cried.

Mom tried scraping off the burned part, but nothing helped. What was left of them was hard as wood. "It's all Jake's fault!" I said, then burst into tears.

"My fault?" the Pain said. "What did I do?"

"He kept distracting me." I could hardly get the words out, I was crying so hard. "That's why I forgot to set the timer. And Charlie doesn't even know how to bake! I had to do everything myself."

"Oh, honey . . ." Mom hugged me. "You must be so disappointed."

"I am. I had it all planned. We were supposed to have ice cream with our cupcakes." I caught the Pain watching me. "Stop staring at me!" I told him.

"I'm not staring."

"Yes, you are!"

"Who'd want to stare at you?"

"We can still have ice cream," Dad said. He opened the freezer and lined up the flavours. "What kind for you, Jake?"

"Why bother to ask him when you already know the answer?" I was sniffling now.

"Abigail . . ." Dad began.

"I'll have vanilla," the Pain told Dad. "The white kind, not the yellow. In a dish, not a cone."

"How unusual," I said.

Dad took a deep breath. "Abigail . . ." he said again.

"Oh, that's right," I said. "The little baby can't have a cone because it's not white!"

This time Dad said, "Abigail . . . we're all sorry about the cupcakes. But remember what we said about being sarcastic?"

Sarcastic is the same as talking *fresh*.

We're not supposed to talk to each other that way because we're a family. The Pain is never *fresh* in front of Mom or Dad. When he feels like dissing me he does it in private. Then he says *ha ha!* I hate hate hate when he says *ha ha!*

Dad handed the Pain a dish of ice cream.

"You're making him into such a baby," I said.

"I'm not a baby!" he shouted.

"Baby is as baby does!" I shouted back. He hates when I call him a baby.

"Abigail, stop this right now," Dad said.

"Why can't he just eat like everyone else?" I asked.

"He will when he's ready," Mom said.

"When will that be? When he's twenty-five? I'll bet he wouldn't have a clue if you blindfolded him and fed him different foods. I'll bet he wouldn't be able to tell what colour food he was eating then."

"Bet I could!" he said.

"OK . . . let's do an experiment," I said. "My science teacher says we should always be looking for experiments we can do at home."

Dad said, "That would be an interesting experiment, but Jake would have to agree."

"I don't agree," he said. "I'm never going to agree!"

"You spoil him because he's the favourite," I cried. "It's disgusting!"

"Oh, honey . . ." Mom said, hugging me again. "You know that's not true. You know we don't have favourites."

"That's what you say, but I can tell you love him best." I felt myself choking up again.

"Abigail, sweetie . . ." Dad said.

The Pain said, "I don't care if you love *her* best, because Fluzzy loves *me* best. So there!" He picked up Fluzzy and let him lick some of his ice cream.

"Fluzzy loves me as much as he loves you!" I shouted.

"Does not!"

"Does too!"

I tried to take Fluzzy away from him. But Fluzzy jumped down and ran around us in circles.

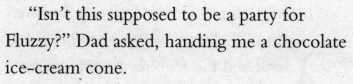

"Isn't this supposed to be a party for Fluzzy?" Dad asked, handing me a chocolate ice-cream cone.

"She ruined the party!" the Pain said, pointing at me. "Her and her stupid cupcakes!"

"What did you say?"

"I *said* you ruined the party crying over your stupid cupcakes. But who cares, because Fluzzy doesn't need a party to know I love him . . . so *ha ha*!"

That did it! I flew across the room and smushed my ice-cream cone against the Pain's forehead. It stuck there. He looked like a unicorn! The ice cream started dripping down his face. When it got to his mouth he stuck out his tongue and lapped it up. "Um . . . good . . ."

"Did you hear that?" I asked Mom and Dad. "It's chocolate! My unicorn is eating *chocolate* ice cream!"

"I'm not your unicorn. I'm your brother! And I'll always be your brother." He grabbed the ice-cream cone off his forehead, took a look, saw that it *was* chocolate, then kept licking it anyway.

"And I'll always be your sister," I told him. "Your *big* sister. And don't you forget it!"

"How could I forget?"

Chocolate
vanilla
Wash
UP

"You can't. Because if it wasn't for me you'd still be eating *vanilla* ice cream!" Now he wasn't just *tasting* my ice cream, he was gobbling it up as fast as he could.

"He's eating my whole ice-cream cone!" I cried.

Mom said, "Don't worry about it." And she made me another one.

After our ice cream we all sang "Happy Birthday" to Fluzzy. And this time when Dad snapped a picture, I think even Fluzzy smiled.

No Hats for Fluzzy

Hats, hats, hats!
Hats for cold white stuff.
Hats for wet stuff.
Hats for riding on wheels.

But no hats for Fluzzy!

She wanted me to wear hats.
That girl with tails coming out of her ears.

I *hissed* to tell her I don't like hats.
But she didn't get it.
She called me *Mister*.
What kind of name is that?
That boy was even worse.
He tried to push me into the bathtub.
Don't you want to learn to swim? he said.
No, I didn't want to learn to swim!
So I *hissed* and I stuck out my claws.

He pulled my tail.
I tried to bite him before he bit me.

They chased me through the house.
Stupid cat! she called.
When the door opened I flew out.
I ran as fast as I could
And as far as I could.
I was never going to let them find me.

When the big booms came I was scared.
But I kept going.
When the sky lit up I shook all over.
But I kept going.
When the water fell from the sky
    I got wet.
But I still kept going.

I kept going until
I was too tired to run any more.
I cried, *Miaow . . . miaow . . .*

A door opened.
I ran inside.
A different boy and girl lived here.
Ohhh . . . he's so wet, she said.
And he's shaking, he said.
Poor little kitty!

They dried me.
They gave me milk
And a soft place to sleep.

When the mom asked,
But who does he belong to?
I didn't tell.
Besides, I never really belonged to those
 other two,
Even if *they* didn't know it.

These two were different.
They called me Fluffy.
Or maybe it was Fuzzy.
No, wait . . . it was *Fluzzy*.
Anything was better than *Mister*.

After that I was happy
Until the cold white day
When I saw *them* again.
Two Tails and *Tail Puller*.

I heard *Two Tails* say, *I know that cat!*
That cat looks just like Mister.

When she said that my fur stood up.
My whiskers stuck out.
Tail Puller said, *Mister was*
a bad cat!

That did it!
I leaped across the
cold white stuff
And crept under the
house.
I didn't come out till I was sure they
were gone.

Tonight when the big booms came again
And the sky lit up
And the water came falling down
I hid in my secret place.

In the closet, right at the back,
On top of the towels.
I didn't come out for a long, long time.

When I did *he* said,
Guess what, Fluzz . . . you're having a party!

Party? I tried to remember what *party* means.
It didn't sound good.

She tried to put a hat on me.
I knew *party* wasn't a good word!
No hats for Fluzzy! I told her.
But *she* didn't get it.
So I shook off the hat.
And I bit it a hundred times.

She said, *Stop that, Fluzzy!*
He laughed.
No hats for Fluzzy! I said again.
This time they understood.
They wore hats, but not me.

When they started fighting about who I
love best
I ran around them in circles.
I love it when they fight over me.

Then I let the two of them stretch me out.
She held my front end.

He held my rear.
I brushed his face with my tail.

They started singing a song.
I think it was about me.
They smiled when the dad snapped
 our picture.
So I smiled too.

I'll stay with them forever.
As long as they remember:
No hats for Fluzzy!

Acknowledgements

With many thanks to Amy Adelson
for sharing her memory of smushing
an ice-cream cone on her brother's forehead.